# The Kiss

Linda Cullen

Attic Press
Dublin

First Published in 1990 by
Attic Press
44 East Essex Street
Dublin 2

British Library Cataloguing in Publication Data
Cullen, Linda
The kiss.
I. Title
823.914 [F]

ISBN 1-85594-002-7

Cover Design: Luly Mason
Origination: Attic Press
Printing: The Guernsey Press Company Ltd.

This book is published with the assistance of The Arts Council / An Chomhairle Ealaíon.

For Tommy and the rest of my very special family,
Mum, Stee, Mark and Dad.
My friends Clodagh, Madeleine, Anne (yes you),
Dermot and Liv who try to keep me sane!
And for Terry - friend and mentor - without whose
encouragement and support this book would not
have been written.

I bet you think I'm mentioning all of you
'cos I'll never write another book?
Wrong!

PS Thank you Attic.

LINDA CULLEN was born in Dublin in 1963 and continues to live there. She has worked as a car driver, a picture framer and was the first freelance camera woman in Ireland. She is now a director, mainly for television.

# Prologue

She sat alone, looking out at the Burren. The two little girls who had self-consciously asked her to 'buy a line' were skipping and singing at the other side of the harbour - stopping at each thatched cottage, reluctantly asking for money for charity. Money, a subject not talked about by the private, modest Irish.

Other than the birds singing the only sound was that of a nearby tractor and an occasional car.

Last month - New York. The month before - Dublin. The month before that - London. Always a city. Always fast. Always loud.

Telephone calls, noisy offices, early morning crew calls. Endless days of meeting new people - big smile - chat - mock, sometimes real, interest. And then the dark, lonely, nonsensical garble of the edit suite. And finally a programme. Sometimes aired, sometimes not. Sometimes good, sometimes not. Occasionally excellent.

The bass tones of male voices interrupted her thoughts. A group of men were standing beside a car dressing themselves. Their canoes were stacked high on a trailer. They were somewhat less self-conscious than the two little girls, she noticed, as their white arses created a defiant glare in her sunglasses.

She picked up her book and concentrated on ignoring the blatant display of locker-room camaraderie before her. Within moments the men were moving off, waving their goodbyes as if there had been some sort of communication.

She could put her book down again. She was trying to 'live for the moment'. Trying not to think of past or future - simply of present. But it was hard. Past, future and present were all bound up with the jet-lagged person who was sleeping soundly in the room upstairs - in the bed they were sharing. She opened the jotter she'd been writing in and read:

*What's in a kiss? Ha - a good question. What is a kiss? Now that's easy. A kiss is a physical exchange between two people. It can be one set of lips pressing against any part of another person. That's a kiss. It can be lips touching lips. That's a kiss too. It can be mouth touching mouth - lips parting - tongue touching tongue - and so on. That is also a kiss.*

*OK, so you knew the answer to that one - big deal. But what about the first one? What's in a kiss? Now, I don't mean saliva or anything like that. I mean what's the big goddamned deal about a kiss? Why does it complicate relationships? Why can't it be just what we said it is - a physical exchange between two people?*

*But it isn't just that.*
*OK - sure - for the moment itself, but it's brought about by an emotional desire - not a physical one.*
*Eureka.*
*Now you might say "why get so complicated about a kiss"? And you may not give a damn. But pay heed because this one particular kiss that happened just a year ago has complicated my life beyond belief.*

She stopped reading and threw her jotter down on the ground. It was getting chilly. The tide was full in now. The little girls long gone home for their tea. And the Complication still sleeping soundly in the attic-like room.

She rubbed her goose-bumped arms. Noticed that the tractor was still going. Stood and walked into the little cottage to light the fire.

The next day they got up late. The Complication feeling rested, they decided to go to the Cliffs of Moher. It was a beautiful day for April - for any time in Ireland really.

The sun was warm as was the breeze. They sat for a long time sheltered by a rock at the top of the cliffs. Sunglasses, jackets, hunkered, protected, silent.

She was thinking - no, not thinking - simply noticing the surrounding beauty. Listening to the faraway waves crashing onto the rocks, the gulls squealing and crying. After a while they left - joking about the possibility of falling and getting killed. Half in earnest. They had tea and scones in a little souvenir shop and felt like tourists, which they weren't. Soul searching not sight-seeing was what they were about. They decided to go to Doolin. They had heard of a 'great pub' there.

She drove and drifted back into her jotter.

*Now you might say that a kiss needn't lead on to anything else and it's only when it does that everything gets complicated. And, well, I'd agree with you. But how do you stop it leading on? That's one question. And the other one is - is it the sex that makes it complicated, not the kiss? But then there wouldn't be the sex without the kiss. Or the kiss without the hug. Or the hug without the touch. Or the touch without the handshake - and the branch on the tree and the tree in the bog and the bog down in the valleyo ...*

She was pulled out of her thoughts by a sign saying *Doolin 2 miles*.

There was a great pub - just as promised. The sun was still shining so everyone was sitting outside. Pints of Guinness, glasses of Guinness, bottles of Guinness. Young foreigners sitting in a circle - one of them with a guitar and a not so good singing voice - the others reading the words to the songs from a battered soodlum book. Only a couple of them noticing the newcomers who sat close but not so close that meant they had to join in.

They straddled the wooden bench facing each other - not touching. There had been an awkward moment earlier when she noticed a gift being worn that hadn't been given by her. Why wear it, she wondered. Had it been to hurt? Why? They were only going to be together for these few days.

It had been removed and explained away as unimportant. The coldness passed and they began to notice the others around them - and enjoy the sunshine, the drink, and the high spirits outside the little pub in Doolin.

That night they went home feeling close and ... happy? Close anyway. They talked. About it all. There was little to be resolved. It had been decided already. Maybe as soon as it began.

They cooked, and opened bottles of wine, trying to maintain the good form of earlier. They succeeded. The fire blazed and the sun went down. The high-ceilinged room grew dark and its inhabitants relaxed. Billie Holliday became a woozy background.

She sat, legs stretched on the soft couch. The Complication was close, cross-legged on a cushion on the floor. They fingered the rims of their glasses and they talked.

Half way through the second bottle of wine the hand that had been resting on her leg reached out and caressed her face. She looked up. Her green eyes met brown and held. Both glasses were placed on the low coffee table. She rested the full of her palm on the Complication's cheek. Brown eyes closed.

"Some things never change do they?" almost whispered.

"No, I suppose they don't," she replied in equal tone.

They remained still for a time and then a thumb moved across her lips - feather-like. They mirrored each other's movements. Gentle hands touched cheeks, lips, hair, eyelids, necks. Outlining each other's faces as if blind. Two hands cupped her face and lips met lips - very gently at first.

The Complication, now kneeling, got up and lay full stretch along her body - still cupping her face - kissing her mouth fully. When the fire had burnt down they went, half naked, up to their bedroom where they took off all their clothes and chains and made love. Slightly drunkenly, slightly desperately. Then to sleep like they used to.

As usual she woke first the next morning. The sun was shining again. She lay on her back, hands cupped behind her head, and counted the rafters on the ceiling - surprised she hadn't counted them already. An arm stretched out and rested across her body.

"Morning."

"Hi there" she smiled, "how are you?"

"Fine. Did you sleep well?"

"Not really" she replied honestly, "how about you?"

"About the same I reckon."

They laughed. She continued counting. The hand that rested on her stomach began to caress her very gently. From her shoulder, lightly over her right breast and down to her stomach. She closed her eyes and her lover continued to touch her - opening the buttons of her nightshirt one by one.

Each caress was like a whisper. She lay still. When she opened her eyes she found brown eyes hovering close - staring - reading.

"Are you OK? Is this OK?"

She hesitated only faintly and said "Yes - it's fine. It's lovely." No smile.

They made love, this time slowly and fully, witnessed only by the stream of light shining through the little attic window.

Later they held each other close and didn't speak for a long time.

They got up and showered together in a haze of soft passion.

* * *

She was quiet during breakfast. Quiet for most of the day. They drove south - to Gort. It was Monday. Two days left. The flight to Hong Kong was on Wednesday morning.

She looked for a bookshop to buy a book for her brother's birthday. No bookshops in Gort. Nothing in Gort - not on a Monday anyway.

They drank tea and coffee in a startlingly clean café and it rained. She had a theory which they discussed at length. About being able to determine a person's character by their career.

She wanted to ask the question but didn't - the question she'd been asking for months.

Why not? Why not be together? They were happy together. They loved each other.

She didn't say it. She was tired of saying it. She was resigned to the fact that this person would walk out of her life in two days and that would be it. There was no coming back.

They found a grocery store open, bought supplies and drove home. In misty Irish rain. Into the cottage. Light the fire.

"Will you read to me?" she asked.

"Sure - you don't want to talk do you?"

"It's not that. Well it is a bit. You don't have to read if you don't want to."

"I'd love to. You know me - love the sound of my own voice."

"I love it too." She let it slip accidentally.

They took up their reading positions. She sat propped against a couple of cushions - her lover, her Complication, sat in between her legs, leaning back into her body.

"You're not to read over my shoulder OK?"

"You always say that and I never do."

"OK, I'd just feel like a terrible idiot if you were miles ahead of me on the page."

"Oh shut up and get on with it would you?" her voice gentle.

They settled themselves and took up from where they'd left off the day before.

The girl left her parents and went to study in London. She met two men - the one she liked was married. She had an affair.

They didn't comment - the story was engrossing.

Occasionally she'd take her hand off her Complication's shoulder and reach over to throw some turf on the fire. It was mild outside and the rain had stopped. They had left the half doors open. The top part swung and creaked. Later, they pulled them closed. Checked they had a key. And walked hand in hand along the water's edge to the pub.

The sun was setting in an orange ball and there was a single swan in the harbour.

"Doesn't she look beautiful," she said.

"Why do you call it a she?"

"Look at it. It couldn't be anything but a she."

The few people there turned their heads away from the fire when they walked in the door. Tweed caps nodded. Irish coffees were the order of the evening.

They sat close on high stools and talked about genders. Time passed quickly and they almost forgot about the dinner they'd left cooking in the oven at home.

It was dark when they left. Dark and cold. They walked fast - arms wrapped around each other, in that awkward-looking way that only lovers seem to manage. They lit candles, threw sods on the fire and sat once again at the low coffee table - eating and drinking and talking. Later when they'd cleared everything away they sat on the couch and kissed. Simple.

Her Complication took both her hands and said "Will anyone ever know you as well as I do?" It was a mistake. She ripped her hands away and stood. Picked up her glass of wine and paced in front of the fire.

"What's wrong? What have I said?"

She screamed suddenly, "What have you said? What have you said? If you feel that - if you know that - if you believe that - that no one will ever know me like you do - then why, why, why are you leaving me? How can you go knowing that? Worse - how can you say it knowing that?"

She turned her back and stared into the fire.

"*Fuck you.*" It came out like an animal's wail. She flung the full glass of wine into the fire. It smashed, flamed and glass ricocheted back into the room. For a moment all she was aware of was the intense heat of the fuelled flame on her face.

Then everything changed with the dying of the flame.

She started to pick up the broken glass.

"Did any of it get you?" she asked.

"No."

"Sorry about that" she said, almost casually. She went into the kitchen and put the glass in the bin. A piece of it nicked her hand. "Ouch."

"Are you hurt?" called in from the sitting-room.

"No - I'm fine."

She dried her hands, walked into the bathroom, picked up a razor and slashed the back of her hand -

twice. Blood oozed slowly from the narrow, straight cuts. She thought it looked like two rivers meeting at a waterfall as she watched the blood spill off her hand onto the floor. She went back into the dark sitting-room, her hand now covered in blood. Invisible without 'night eyes'.

Her Complication moved warily towards her.

"Jesus Christ! What happened? You're covered in blood." A towel was grabbed from the back of a chair and wrapped gently around her hand.

"You said you weren't cut. Are you alright?"

She didn't reply - just looked at the red stain blotting the white towel.

"Oh no - oh God, you did it yourself." The towel had been removed to examine the damage. "Please don't do this. Not again. Please. I'm sorry - I'm so sorry. I didn't realise."

She watched numbly as tears spilled out of the brown eyes she knew so well.

That night she got into bed, carefully observed, bandaged, exhausted. She woke up screaming from a nightmare and was held tight. She saw things in the dark so the light was left on. Her dreams were of crumbling stairs and blood and circles.

She was woken by a hand on her cheek.

"It's a beautiful morning - are you alright?"

"I'm fine" she said, rubbing the sleep from her eyes.

"Don't wake up too much. I just wanted to tell you I'm going out for a walk."

"Do you want me to come."

"No thanks - it's alright."

"Are you sure?" She opened her eyes.

"Positive - really - I'd prefer to go alone."

She drifted back into a light sleep and didn't come to until an hour later when she heard the front door close and a poker clanking in the grate. She remained silent - looking at the dust particles floating in the path of sunlight which passed above her head and landed on the armchair at the end of the bed. Faded denims, her favourite jumper, socks. All of them leaving tomorrow.

Fully awake she called "Hi there."

"Oh I'm sorry, did I wake you?"

"No, I was awake already."

She got out of bed and put on her robe - opened the bedroom door and leant on the bannisters.

"Did you have a good walk?"

"Yes - lovely."

"Are you working?"

"Yes. I've a special lecture to prepare for Thursday."

"Oh." Never any doubt about the departure so. Never.

She went downstairs, made tea and coffee for both of them, sat in an armchair and picked up her jotter.

*So we've covered kissing - sort of. Time to move on. To platonic relationships. Now there's a goodie. Some people say there is no such thing. And I used to say "Pah - ridiculous" but is it? Is it really so ridiculous? I'm beginning to wonder. No point in wondering really. How can anyone be truly objective about something they're so involved in? Oh no - not another question. I used to think I was the Queen of Objectivity. But then, I used to think a kiss was a physical exchange. That boundaries were the same as barriers. And that relationships could be platonic.*

Their last full day together.

They walked on the vast beach in Lahinch, bought ice-cream cones, donned sunglasses and looked like tourists.

The sea was calm and the sand hard. There were people dotted all the way along the beach. They walked until they found a comfortable rock - one with a body curve - and they lay back drinking in the mild sunshine.

"Let's find somewhere really good to eat tonight," she suggested. "And let's sort out anything we need to now - quickly - who tells who and all that stuff."

She couldn't help thinking it was like a ludicrously friendly divorce. Without the marriage. There could never have been a marriage.

That done they went in search of a good restaurant - in vain. They ended up buying favourite foods and wines and eating in again. As they were walking back to the car, she noticed it wasn't where she'd parked it.

"Where's the car?" she asked, not quite believing her eyes.

"Oh my God. It's gone."

They looked at each other and burst out laughing - in the middle of the street in Lahinch - with people staring at them as if they were demented.

The car wasn't gone. A farmer had taken the handbrake off and pushed it down the road, away from his gateway.

It was a mild evening and they left the half doors open again as they cooked and listened to music.

Their humours matched. Calm and sad. They smiled and touched often. They drank quickly to ease the sadness. And made love a little bit like the first night - desperately.

They woke to an alarm for the first time since arriving. They hugged close and tight. Made love for the last time and got up quickly. Avoiding each other's eyes. It was a grey day. They assumed separate household tasks and cleared up within an hour. When she went outside to empty the ashes it started to lash rain. She stood still, holding the bucket in her hand, her hair and clothes getting drenched - and she cried.

They drove to Shannon in almost total silence. Noticing silently that they'd never finished the book.

The flight was boarding when they arrived.

"I'll always love you, you know that don't you?"

"Yes, I think I do," she replied through tears.

She watched her lover walk through the barrier. The walk and the back that were so familiar to her turned and waved.

The rain had stopped and the sun was breaking through the clouds when she got into her car to drive back home.

# Chapter One

*Get up, get up, get up you lazy donkey,*
*Get up, get up, get up you sleepy head,*
*Get up, get up, get up you lazy donkey,*
*You lazy donkey, get out of bed.*

The blankets were pulled up over her head, and she was singing very quietly underneath them. Her right foot swung in rhythm with the song as she edged outwards - seeing how far she had to move before her big toe touched the floor.

"Joanna, are you up yet?" her mother impatiently called from downstairs. "You'll be late."

She flung the blankets back, rolled over suddenly and landed on all fours - then pounded the floor with her hands shouting, "I'm up, I'm up - nearly dressed Mum - down in a second."

Within minutes she was studying herself in the full-length mirror on the landing.

Grey skirt - too long. White blouse - startling. Grey jumper - too big and itching her wrists. Black lace-up shoes - still black at the toes. And grey knee socks.

"Yuk," she made a face at herself, then pulled the tops of her socks outwards until she felt the elastic in them break.

"That's better," she said as they fell down around her ankles.

She bounded down the stairs, counting as she ran.

"Porridge, Pet?" her father asked.

"No thanks Daddy." She poured herself some cornflakes and wondered why he always asked her did she want some porridge - she hated porridge.

"You look very grown-up in your uniform. Doesn't she, boys?"

"Mmm," Rory, her eldest brother muttered - not looking at her. Their uniforms were almost identical, except Rory and Conor were wearing red ties and long grey trousers. They were unremarkably good-looking boys - brown hair, blue eyes, regular features - neat. Twelve and thirteen. She was almost four years younger - reddish untidy hair (kept short to keep in order), a pug nose, green eyes, and small. She was very small.

Her mother came into the kitchen with her coat on, carrying her 'magic bag'. The ugly thing that held everything imaginable in it. She looked like her mother.

"Stand up and let me see you."

She stood to be inspected. Her mother bent down and pulled up the socks.

"You look grand. Now don't be nervous today - don't

worry about anything. You'll manage fine. I'll see you this evening and you can tell me all about it."

"OK Mum."

"Eat your cornflakes."

"They're soggy."

"You should have eaten them before they got soggy."

"The milk was warm."

"Sometimes you make no sense, Child" she said, obviously aggravated.

Joanna sat again as her mother left the house in a whirlwind, calling goodbyes, issuing instructions, planting kisses on three foreheads and picking up things on her way out the door.

The only sound when she left were Joanna's feet tapping on the lino floor. She toyed with her cornflakes and smiled to herself as her socks fell back down around her ankles.

Her first day in her new school had been fine. She made a friend, liked her teacher, loved the playground and could find nothing to be nervous about. The school was very different to her old one. Here there were nuns and no boys. She missed her friend Joe, but it was OK because the other new girl that day, Helen, played with her at break-time.

Joanna was hanging upside-down on the monkey-puzzle with her eyes closed and her hands over her ears. Helen spotted her and pulled at her arm. She opened her eyes and laughed.

"What are you laughing at?"

"You - you look funny upside-down."

Helen didn't laugh. "What are you doing?"

"Listening," Joanna replied closing her eyes again.

"Listening to what?"

"Everything."

"What do you mean?"

She opened her eyes again, "Come up here and I'll show you."

"Do I have to hang upside-down?" Helen asked warily.

"Of course you do - it doesn't work otherwise - come on."

"But what about my skirt?"

"What about it?"

"It'll fall down like yours and show off my knickers."

"Oh! - I didn't notice it coming loose," said Joanna. "Just do this," she gathered the end of her skirt and tucked it into the legs of her knickers. "See, they're just like shorts now."

Very seriously, Helen copied her new friend and climbed up beside her.

When they were both hanging side by side like bats, Joanna said, "Now press your hands against your ears - really hard - and then let them go again. Do it really fast. Don't forget to close your eyes. And keep on doing it."

Helen did what she was told and listened to the dreamy, wave-like sound it produced. A sound that got more intense the longer you hung upside-down.

"Well?" Joanna asked, "whaddayathink?"

"It's great."

She closed her eyes again and Joanna sang a long note of "Helen" into her ear so it sounded like "Helen-en-en-en-en."

They both started to laugh.

After break that day they were summoned to the head nun's office.

Joanna knocked on the door. Her small knuckles made little impression on the heavy, dark wood. She knocked again, harder this time.

"Come in," Sister Mary's voice called.

They sidled in and stood with their backs to the door. Sister Mary sat behind a huge desk on a brown leather swivel chair. The leather was wrinkled, like her skin. She had a small face and small eyes. She was caressing two pink bands that were on her desk.

"Which one of you knocked on the door?" she asked smiling at them.

"I did," replied Joanna.

"I did, what?" said the nun.

"Knock on the door."

"No child - not 'I did knock on the door' but, 'I did, *Sister*'."

"Oh I'm sorry - Sister."

"Good girl. Now there is never any need to knock on my door twice. I have perfect hearing. Just wait until I am ready. Is that understood?" She was still smiling.

"Yes Sister."

"Now children" she stood up, holding the pink bands. She was very tall and droopy, a bit like a weeping willow. "These pink ribbons are very important. You will have noticed most of the other girls wearing them. The girls that are not wearing them are in disgrace. These ribbons differentiate between good girls and bad girls." She continued stroking the bands as she came from behind her desk. "If a girl is bad her ribbon will be removed from her at assembly on Friday, in front of the entire school, by Mother Superior. It will not be returned until the girl has prove that she is sorry and will never repeat the bad deed." She looked from girl to girl. "Do you understand the importance of these ribbons?"

"Yes Sister" they chorused.

She placed the first pink ribbon on Helen. It went over her left shoulder and was tied in a bow at her right hip.

After giving Joanna hers she excused them telling them they were very welcome and not to forget to keep the precious pink ribbons "spotlessly clean."

After that they made up a new game in the playground. They would count how many ribbon-less girls there were and then try to guess what dreadful thing they had done.

* * *

German Jumps and the new decimal system were the major concerns that year. Joanna had no problem mastering the German Jumps. The decimal system was a bit tougher.

"So, one old penny is the same as one new penny except for the size," Joanna said to Rory one evening when he was helping her out with her homework.

"No Joanna - you're not listening. They're called the same thing but they have different values as well as looking different. One new penny is worth more than two old pennies."

"Well then, why isn't it called 2p?"

"Because it isn't - this is the new system."

"Well, why do they have a new system? What's wrong with the old one? I think it's all stupid."

"I think you're stupid and I can't be bothered helping you any more. I've got my own homework to do."

Later, when her mother came in from work she asked her about the new 'demical' system.

"It's 'decimal' pet" her mother replied and told her to ask Rory or Conor for help.

* * *

"Rory, Rory" she poked her brother through the covers. He was asleep. "Rory, wake up - I'm scared" she whispered urgently, "Rory," she shook him harder.
He sat up suddenly.

"What? What's the matter?" he asked, blinking his eyes.

"I'm scared."

"Scared of what?"

"There's someone *breathing* in my room."

"Not again Joanna."

"But this time there really is. I think it's coming from the cupboard."

"Did you check the cupboard before you went to bed, like I told you to?"

"Yes Rory." She couldn't hold the tears back any longer. "But I'm sure there's someone there now" she sobbed. "I'm cold Rory."

Rory felt sorry for her, standing there in her cotton nightshirt with the cuffs pulled over her hands and grabbed tight in each one.

"Get in." He threw back the covers and moved over. Her face broke into a smile at her luck and she jumped into the bed before he had a chance to change his mind like Conor usually did. Sometimes she went to everyone's bedside frightened and ended up having to go back to the breathing room.

Turning his back to her he said "Not a word now Joanna, just go asleep, OK? Have we got a deal?"

"Yes Rory."

"Night Joanna."

"Night Rory."

There was a moment's silence.

"Rory?" she whispered.

"What?" Sharply - she was pushing her luck.

"There it is again - can't you hear it - the *breathing*."

"That's Conor you twit" he snapped at her.

"Oh, I'm sorry."

She tried to make out her other brother, but could barely see his form in the other bed.

"Rory, can I get in the inside - please?" she said very quickly.

"Oh God, alright. But one more sound and I'm serious - you'll be back in your own room."

She clambered over him and settled between his back and the wall. She felt safer there. No hands could come up from under the bed and grab her - except maybe from the bottom of the bed.

She scrunched her legs up against her belly hurriedly at the thought. She put her face under the covers and her thumb in her mouth and thought to herself that Rory wouldn't call her a twit if he knew what it meant. Someone had told her it was a very rude word - it meant a pregnant camel. She decided she should wait and tell him in the morning.

"Thank you, Rory" she whispered as she was drifting off.

* * *

At the end of the year Helen's family moved away - to another country - Africa. Helen's father was a foreign something or other. They had been travelling since before Helen was born. This time they'd be away for four years.

They promised to write to each other 'every week', which of course they didn't. Joanna made new friends.

They sent Christmas cards the first year - spurred on by their parents. That was all. Joanna had other things on her mind.

Two terrible things happened.

She lost her pink ribbon - and her father.

* * *

With Helen gone she didn't bother with German Jumps any more. She had a new friend, and a new game.

Her friend was called Fiona, who thought that hanging upside-down on the monkey-puzzle and screaming was childish. She was tall and quiet and thought Joanna loud. Joanna thought her friend was sort of sophisticated. For some odd reason they got along really well. And the new game. The new game was 'clackers'. It was the rage. Both girls took to it quickly and could do almost anything with them. The playground looked and sounded like a mass of colourful foreign insects. Bright orange balls that looked as if they were flying. And sounded more obvious than crickets at night in some foreign land. Joanna knew about crickets from TV.

At break-time every little girl pulled her clackers out of her schoolbag, held them quietly and walked along the left hand side of the corridor into the playground. And then it started. As sudden as a balloon bursting.

Dozens of smiling grey-clad, pink-ribboned little girls ran to 'their' area in the playground - and 'clacked' and showed off and counted. The monkey-puzzle and the big slide were completely neglected.

One day, approaching break-time, Joanna spotted Mona (a new girl she didn't like) doing something with her bag.

"What are you doing?" Joanna asked.

Mona was surprised at being seen and her pale freckled face blushed red.

"Nothing," she replied.

Joanna put her sewing into her bag and pulled out her clackers. But the orange balls didn't follow the string she was pulling. They'd been cut off.

Mona began to laugh.

Joanna screamed at her. "*You bitch.*" She didn't know what it meant, and was so raging that she didn't care - she just knew it was bad.

The class went as silent as if Mother Superior had walked in. Some of them had never heard the word before.

Miss O'Brien stood with her hand frozen on the door handle. The only person unaware of all this was an enraged and screaming Joanna, who was shaking off Fiona's restraining hand.

"Look Fiona, look what she's done."

Miss O'Brien roared "Joanna!"

Joanna turned to her, almost annoyed at the interruption.

"Yes Miss?"

"Come with me immediately. We are going to see Sister Mary."

"But what about *her*?" She almost spat the 'her'. "She cut my clackers."

"I don't care Joanna. Nothing can excuse the language I have just heard coming out of your mouth."

Joanna followed quietly, but angrily, clackers in hand.

Sister Mary had plenty to say. And said it all without raising her voice. She threw Joanna's clackers in the bin, forbidding her to get a new set, and told her to be quiet. She was always "far too outspoken" for her own good.

"Come with me."

She led Joanna to the school chapel and put her kneeling outside the doors. "You are dismissed from class for the day - and you will kneel here and pray until it is time to go home."

Joanna knelt on the cold hard marble, truly quiet now.

"Ask God for his forgiveness Child, because now you are not worthy to be inside his house. That is why you are here."

Joanna could feel tears coming to her eyes so she kept her head bent. As the nun left she pulled at the shoulder of her pink ribbon.

"I hope you're not too fond of this?" she said before leaving her.

Every half hour someone was sent to check on her. And if she was on her hunkers she was told to kneel up straight. She was too frightened to get up and walk around so she didn't. She spent her time counting the little stained glass windows. And then counting the different colours. And then counting the footsteps of her gaolers. She thought it would never end. She tried counting her pulse but couldn't find it and for a moment thought she might be dying until she found her heartbeat and counted that instead.

At three o'clock Sister Mary came to tell her she could go. When she stood, her knees buckled under her and she fell. She smiled a little remembering what her Dad always said about her not having far to fall, and stood again. Sister Mary caught the smile and made no move to help her.

That night she waited until her mother was alone and told her the whole story - including what she said.

"Don't cry Joanna - don't cry. I know you're good and God knows you're good too."

But Joanna cried bitterly because it didn't really matter if her mother and God thought she was good. It was Sister Mary and Mother Superior who mattered. They were in control of the pink ribbons.

Friday and assembly came slowly.

Each class had different seats in the huge hall. And in the centre of the circles of chairs sat Mother Superior - all in black - at a desk. She was so old she looked like what Joanna imagined dead people must look like. And on the desk in front of her was a list of all the girls. Starting with the oldest class, down to the youngest. Joanna was low on the list. She was ten.

Beside the lists were four sets of cards - in different colours. Pink for excellent. Red for very good. Blue for good. And a sort of off-white for satisfactory.

She kept pulling up her socks waiting for her class names to begin. The middle classes were all walking up to the old nun, curtseying and receiving their merit cards. Her class was next. She was sixth on the roll.

"Jane Kearns - excellent. Mary Keating - excellent. Mary Mahoney - very good. Judith Manning - excellent." They were all standing, ready to approach the desk. "Jennifer Malloy - very good." A slight pause. "Maire O'Sullivan ..." And on and on.

She didn't really hear the rest. She'd been skipped. She sat alone shivering while the rest of her class got their merits, including Mona. The worst was yet to come. After the eight year-olds had been called the hall applauded. Her hands were freezing, even though she was sitting on them. She was shaking.

"Girls." Sister Mary said loudly from beside Mother Superior. "We have two disappointments this week. And they are, Jacintha O'Mahony - a senior. And Joanna Maloney - a junior."

You could have heard a pin drop, if one had bothered dropping. But not for long because the girl who had to be Jacintha burst out crying. Joanna followed her to the desk - 150 pairs of eyes followed too. Jacintha took off her ribbon and laid it down on the desk. Joanna did the same - tears still not falling. She felt as if there was a hand wrapped around her throat.

When eventually they filed out of the hall, she ran into the toilet and vomited.

A few weeks later one of the girls got a broken nose from her clackers and they were banned.

The only reminder was a set that had been thrown so high they got caught in the telephone wires above the playground. For years after that they could be heard clacking on a windy day.

* * *

Around that time Joanna started to keep a diary. Well it wasn't a diary exactly. It was in fact a jotter and on the outside she wrote: *Private Property - Do Not Read.* Oddly she never dated anything she wrote.

*My ribbon was taken away today because I called Mona a terrible name. I didn't mean to really. It just came out. She cut my clackers and now I'm not allowed have new ones. I hate Mona. Then I got sick and Daddy wasn't there when Sister Mary rang to ask him to take me home so she had to ring Mummy at work and then Mummy and Daddy had a big fight so I didn't get into trouble about losing my ribbon.*

The following week she got her ribbon back - vowing never to behave in such a disgraceful way again. Its disappearance and reappearance went unremarked by her whole family.

She became a little quieter in school, paying heed to what Sister Mary had said. And she went into the little chapel every day - to ask God for his forgiveness.

* * *

It was nearing the end of that school year when she came home from school one day and there was no one in. She dropped her schoolbag at the front door and clambered over the shed roof, onto the oil tank, down the lilac tree, in the sitting-room door, through to the front door and picked up her bag.

She thought it all very exciting and went up to the attic, her Dad's workshop, to check if he was there and just hadn't heard her.

His high swivel stool was empty. The familiar slanted drawing board was there with a large sheet of white paper on top. Pencil lines all over it. A house plan for the Gorman's, she knew. It was her Dad's latest big job.

For the past week she had sat up on the other high stool, after school, beside her Dad. Watching him draw his precise lines with a ruler. Always sitting back and squinting after each stroke.

She made him cups of tea, which he always re-made. Never telling her why. She wished she knew because she'd be able to 'not do' whatever it was he didn't like.

He was a tall man, with blue eyes and darker brown hair than her brothers. He always wore trousers and a tie. She thought it was strange because he didn't have to go to his office any more. Especially since he didn't see anyone except her all day. But each morning he got up and put on a fresh shirt, suit trousers and a tie. She preferred the weekends when he wore jeans.

She always knew how to behave with him - when to talk or not. When she was chattering too much (and she knew she did because her teachers often called her a chatterbox) he would reach across and put his hand on her knee - gently. Then she'd be quiet and just watch the hand take up its pencil and draw its neat lines. His fingers were long and sallow-skinned, with dark hairs on the back of them. Sometimes she tried to count the hairs but never managed to. She always began talking before the end. It was part of their routine. To sit and talk while he worked. Then at five they'd go downstairs together, light the fire and prepare the dinner. Rory and Conor came in around that time, but just to change before going out again.

But that day he wasn't there. She was delighted. She ran back downstairs and cleaned out the grate, setting the firelighters and briquettes neatly in it. Taking care not to spill any, she put the hot ashes out in the tin in the back garden. She didn't light the fire. She wasn't allowed to. She went into the kitchen, washed the breakfast things and peeled the potatoes - on her tiptoes. When her father came home she was sitting at the table with a cup of tea and a comic in hand. She felt very grown-up.

"Sorry I wasn't here when you got home Pet - I was with Mr Gorman. He wanted to see how I was doing with the house plans."

"That's OK, Daddy" she was smiling from ear to ear waiting for him to notice all the work she'd done. He went upstairs.

A few minutes later she went up after him to tell him he could work a little later on the Gorman's plans as everything was ready. She was practically bursting to tell him. He hugged her. And she wondered how he made such big photocopies of his plans to show his clients because surely he didn't draw everything twice!

She got used to these days.

She wasn't supposed to answer the front door unless she knew who was there. But she thought that was silly and rude because the door was made of clear glass and you could see right through it. Both ways. So if she looked to see who was there, they'd know she was in anyway!

One day she was lying on the sitting-room floor reading the *Tammy* and there was a loud hammering. She jumped. Everyone rang the bell! The hammering continued as she edged her way along the sitting-room wall, under the front window, to the hallway.

She got down on her hands and knees to peer around the corner. She had often imagined this happening and had decided that if she looked from the floor she'd be at a different eye-level and the person wouldn't see her.

But this person did.

The big burly man - older, fatter and greyer than her Dad, stopped hammering and looked straight into the little green, staring, ten year-old eyes.

"I'm looking for your father," he shouted through the door.

She felt silly on her hands and knees so she stood up, staring back at him thinking "If I say he's in he'll want to see him, and I can't say he isn't in." She was torn.

"I'm looking for Gordon Maloney - is he in?" He was beginning to sound cross.

She didn't move.

Suddenly the man smiled.

"I'm a friend of his. I'm from the police station."

Her face cracked with relief. She went to the door, stretched up and undid the latch.

"He's not here right now. Do you want to leave a message? He'll be home soon." Just like she said on the telephone.

"What's your name little one?" He sounded nicer now and had crouched down to her level. She could smell his after-shave - it made her gag a bit.

"Joanna." She replied.

"Well Joanna, are you here on your own?"

All warnings about door openings rushed back into her head. Her Dad would be so annoyed when he heard about this. What could she say? He had told her never to say she was alone - even to her Mum when she phoned.

Before she could answer the man stood to his full height and said "Don't worry Joanna - just tell that father of yours Jim from the station called. Tell him I want to see him. Will you do that?"

She nodded.

"Now close the door and don't open it again until he comes home."

She closed the door firmly behind his heavy frame and heavy smell and worried about what her Dad would say to her.

He didn't seem to mind at all. He went upstairs to the workshop and closed the door.

* * *

"Bam" the front door closed. Eleven forty five pm Tuesday.

"Creak" the sitting-room door opened.

Silence.

And closed.

"One, two, three, four, five," cigarette smoke smell - breathe deeply - "six, seven, eight, nine, ten. There they go."

She lay face down and pulled her pillow over her head, pushing it round her ears.

If she pressed really hard she could hear nothing, but if she let the pressure up a bit she could hear them shouting. Always the same things. And she noticed that adults went on and on about the same things, just like children were always accused of doing.

He always came into her room at night to tuck her in - often with a grease-stained bag of soggy chips. He'd sit at the edge of her bed and they'd eat the chips together, her telling him about her day. Then he'd crumple up the empty bag, take aim, and throw it across the room into the bin. He never missed.

He'd kiss her on the forehead and switch off the light leaving her to snuggle down, put her thumb in her mouth, crook her finger around her nose and fall into a deep sleep with the comforting smells of chips and cigarette smoke still in the room. The last thing she'd hear was her father saying goodnight to the boys.

More and more often her Dad wasn't in when she came home from school. Mostly she saw him when he said goodnight to her. He didn't have breakfast with them any more. And when he was in they just fought. Her Mum and Dad. Their voices would start off low and sort of cold.

"Where have you been?"

"Out."

"Out where?"

"It doesn't matter where - just out."

"You weren't here when Joanna came home from school again today."

His voice would get louder now.

"I was trying to get some work to support us, Anne."

"Well you're not doing such a good job of it are you Gordon?" Her mother never shouted. "Look at these - the electricity is going to be cut off. I'm going to have to ask Michael for a loan again."

"You *will not* ask your brother for money to pay my bills."

"Well how in God's name will we pay them if I don't - my salary barely covers the food."

"You know I've got an interview next week. Just leave it be until we see if I get the job - OK? We'll manage."

"We won't manage and you know it."

And it would go on and on. Almost always about money.

One night during one of the fights her mother went to the phone saying, "Look Gordon, it's going to be cut off tomorrow if I don't get some money from Michael. You can't work from home without a phone."

She picked up the phone and began to dial her brother's number.

"Put down the phone Anne," he said very quietly. She continued to dial.

Suddenly, he jumped up and roared, "I said put down the fucking phone Anne." He tore the phone out of her hand and pushed her against the wall, slamming the phone back into place at the same time.

Her mother paled and kept herself pressed hard against the kitchen wall. She looked terrified. Her father stood glaring at her, his knuckles white, still grasping the phone.

Joanna ran out of the kitchen and up to her bedroom. The boys had left as soon as the argument began.

One morning Rory woke her instead of her Mum.

"Joanna, get up - it's time for school."

She rubbed the sleep out of her eyes. He was at the end of her bed holding her toes. She pulled her foot away.

"Come on. We're all late."

"Why? Where's Mummy?"

"She's not well, she's in bed."

She got up and dressed for school hurriedly. She didn't need to pull the tops of her socks out any more. They all fell down around her knees anyway.

There was no one to offer her porridge that morning. She got her own cornflakes and sat with her silent brothers.

"Where's Daddy?" She asked.

"Gone," said Rory, not looking up from his toast.

"Gone where?" she asked.

"Gone away."

"Where?" she was truly curious now.

"Gone away - from here - for good, Joanna."

"What do you mean 'gone for good'. He can't be. Where would he go?" She was worried now.

"Look Joanna, he's gone away - from us - to... I don't know where, and he's not coming back."

She said nothing.

She looked at her brother, her eyes glistening with tears and started to scream: "Tell me where he is and I'll get him back - tell me Rory? He'll come home if I ask him. Tell me."

She was crying, pulling at his jumper. He was looking back at her, sort of blankly. He didn't even try to stop her pounding his arm with her angry little fists.

Conor picked up her still full bowl of soggy cornflakes and brought them over to the sink.

"Tell me Rory, tell me." She was tiring now.

"I don't know Joanna. I don't know."

"Mummy must know - I'll ask her." She moved to the kitchen door.

Rory lashed out like an unleashed spring and grabbed her arm. "Don't Joanna. Don't go near her."

She went and sat at the clear front door, on her red stool, grey coat belted around her, schoolbag at her feet. And she waited until the McGrath's silver car pulled up outside and beeped before she had time to wave.

It was the same as every day - of every week - of every month - of every year. The only difference being that she jumped up and left the house unkissed.

* * *

And so it was each morning until she was old enough to cycle to school.

She never told Fiona, or any of her friends, about her Daddy. She just never asked them to come home with her after school and at weekends.Her Mum gave her a note for Sister Mary a few weeks later. Sister Mary read it carefully. Joanna didn't know what it said. She just noticed the teachers treating her differently after. Some paid her more attention - others, less. And the following morning Sister Mary announced a special prayer at assembly for Joanna Maloney and her family. Joanna pinched herself to check she was still alive. They only said special prayers for dead people.

She thought it was strange that Fiona didn't pair up with her for skipping that day - no one did in fact.

That year, she began her second jotter.

# Chapter Two

*They say he fancies you - so he must. Don't ask me how he could, but he does. I realise they may be lying, but why would your best friends lie to you - serio? So get your act together and go to that party and go for it. He's good looking and nice. And he likes you. He does - really.*

She closed her seventh jotter.

She was just fifteen.

"Mum, can I go to a party on Saturday night?"

"A party?" Her mother looked up from her paper. "Whose?"

"Paul O'Mahony's"

"Do I know him?"

"I don't think so. He's Kathy's cousin. They live in Ballybrack."

"Well, how will you get home?"

Easy - she had it sussed. A pushover. "Kathy's Dad is picking us up. In fact I'm going straight over to Kathy's when I finish work. Jenny and Maire are meeting us there later."

"OK Pet." Her mother went back to her newspaper.

Joanna had taken on a job in a local newsagent to give herself pocket money. She knew how hard it was for her Mum to get enough money to keep the house going, never mind having to clothe her too. Recently, though, she was glad to see her Mum not doing so much overtime. Conor and Rory had both left school and Conor was working as a mechanic in a garage. He adored cars and was always coming home with some half wrecked, souped-up car with spoilers and stripes and furry dice. It was strange, she thought, that she and Conor got on so well - not she and Rory. Rory had always been the one who took care of her when she was a child, but when their father left he seemed to change. He never let her into his bed at night after that - no matter how scared she was. It was always Conor. Rory had done well in his leaving certificate. Her mother was always telling uncle Michael how bright he was when Michael was giving out about Rory being on the dole.

"Michael - don't get at him. It's difficult for him. He's not like Conor. He wouldn't be able for the bank or the civil service or whatever. It would kill him. He needs more freedom."

"He needs a kick up the backside if you ask me. And if I was his father I'd give him one."

Her mother would respond coldly, "You're not his father Michael - I am however, his mother, and I will deal with Rory as I see fit."

She'd soften slightly then. "Look Michael, I really appreciate all the help you've given me over the years. Really I do. I couldn't have managed without you. But leave the kids out of it will you? Surely you've enough to deal with with your own?"

Joanna couldn't stand her three cousins. All girls, younger than her. She just about tolerated her severe, balding uncle because she knew he helped them out financially.

She made fun of him. It was her way of dealing with his seriousness.

He was oddly fond of Joanna because of this.

Conor was always friendly - to everyone. Distant, but friendly.

Rory? Rory wouldn't even look up from a book whenever Michael walked into the house. Sometimes he'd even get up and walk out of the room.

* * *

Joanna, Kathy, Jenny, Maire. Friends. All in the same class in school. All in Lois denims, bright sweatshirts and brown leather boots.

In Kathy's beforehand they brushed hair, put on clear lipgloss and prided themselves in the fact they didn't need to wear makeup - they examined their images, very briefly, in the mirror. Vanity was not tolerated amongst this group.

Joanna looked at her friends, seeing their attractiveness, then she stared again into her own eyes and wondered why Geoff liked her. She didn't like what she saw. Pale. Skinny. Sharp. She pulled her finger along her cheek and chin. Her skin was a mess too.

'No accounting for people's taste' she sighed, but smiled as she turned from the mirror.

It was the first real mixed party they'd ever been to.

Paul's older sister opened the door and led them down to the basement where they could hear voices and loud, loud pulsating music.

Joanna stood between her friends who nudged her sharply when Geoff noticed her coming in the door. She looked away embarrassed.

There were few people she didn't recognise there. The 'Ride of Rock' was talking to a dark-haired girl beside the stereo. He was a friend of Geoff's. She didn't like him. Thought him bigheaded.

She danced and flirted, as best she knew how. And was cool (she thought) when Geoff finally asked her to dance.

'Freebird' was playing. He was a good foot taller than her and had dark curly hair and grey eyes. She liked his eyes but was afraid to look at them. He liked her hair and smile but didn't tell her.

And so they danced, arms awkwardly wrapped around one another, each savouring the other's unfamiliar smell.

Hesitation then as the song became fast. They looked around to see if the other couples were dancing fast or what - caught each other and laughed. Jimmy 'the Ride' was sitting in a corner with his dark girlfriend kissing her. His hands were on her breasts. Joanna was shocked. Geoff noticed her look and blushed. They both blushed and then he kissed her.

There was neither awkwardness nor experience in that kiss.

It was ... nice.

He asked to walk her home and she said yes.

Jenny came up and whispered that 'they made a lovely couple' in her ear and she blushed even more.

They were walking home with Jimmy and his girl too. She smiled at the dark-haired girl as Jimmy introduced her.

"Joanna this is Helen."

It registered with them both at the same time.

Helen - her friend from junior school who'd hung upside-down on the monkey puzzle! Who'd gone away for years and years.

Joanna spoke first. "I lost my pink ribbon after you left you know."

They both laughed and the boys were sorry they'd decided to go home in a foursome as they walked a few steps behind the two girls deep in conversation.

* * *

Joanna and Geoff became a couple.

They met every day after school. At first shyly. And then surely. And they discovered each other's brains and bodies. Well, explored rather than discovered.

Geoff came to her home mostly and he knew about Joanna's father. He didn't mind. He understood. His mother was dead.

She fell in love with Geoff and he with her. And accidentally she forgot to put the dinner on in time and light the fire.

But that was mostly because she and Helen were talking, endlessly, at the Harbour - about Geoff and whoever else. They went different directions after the pier, so they'd drop their bikes there and sit on the wooden bench at the corner. Talking, talking, talking. Helen even knew about her father.

"They're all going away for two weeks at Christmas."
"Who?"
"Geoff and his Dad and his brothers"
"Really! You'll miss him."
"Yes, I suppose so."
"Are you staying faithful?"
"Oh God yes - of course."
"But two weeks, It's a long time. Will he be faithful?"
"He'd better be."

She didn't miss him as much as she thought she should. She felt lonely on Christmas day when she had a special present left under the tree for her. A bottle of perfume and a pressed red rose.

She told Helen about the perfume but not the rose.

She didn't tell her that is, until they were lying side by side on the pull-out couch in front of the fire - talking until the early hours. Until Joanna's mother called into them that it was time to sleep.

Then, they told each other everything. They would lie on their backs - sleeping bag underneath, duvet on top, nightdress on Joanna and whatever old T-shirt available on Helen, and watch the flickering light from the fire on the ceiling. Hands folded on stomachs. Eyes wide. Minds deep in thought. Bodies relaxed. Whispering.

"What do you think of sex before marriage Helen?"

Helen turned on her side suddenly. "Oh my God - you're not going to are you?"

"Don't be ridiculous" Joanna laughed. "I'm only just sixteen."

"But he wants to doesn't he?"

"No - Helen now stop it. Just tell me what you

think?"

"OK - I've thought about it a lot." She reverted to lying on her back. "I know it's wrong - in the eyes of the church, and our parents. But how can you decide to live with someone forever if ..." she looked at Joanna, "you've never been to bed with them."

They both giggled.

"Shhhhh" said Joanna.

"Well what do you think?"

"Oh - pretty much the same - but there's something else too."

"What?"

"I don't really understand why some things are OK and others aren't."

"What do you mean?"

"I mean, it's wrong to have sex - sexual intercourse," she found the words hard to say, "before marriage, but it's fine to do ... other things."

Helen thought for a moment.

"I don't think it is ... fine to do other things. In the eyes of the church."

"No - I know." Joanna said quickly. "I know it isn't in the eyes of the church. But everyone seems to make such a big deal about - losing this virginity, and all, and I don't really see what the big difference is between that and everything else everyone gets up to. I think it's hypocritical."

Helen smiled. "Yes - I know what you mean. Jenny is always saying she'll be a virgin when she gets married and all that crap, and yet you and me both know what she and Jason get up to in his little Fiat Bambino."

"Exactly" Joanna replied.

They fell asleep that night, like most nights, facing each other, feet entwined, in mid-sentence, the fire dead.

* * *

Geoff was eighteen and a virgin. Unlike most of his friends. Certainly unlike his best friend Jimmy who'd lost his virginity 'hundreds of times'. He was studying for his leaving certificate and wanted to be a doctor like his father.

He had never felt so distracted from his books as now.

He and Joanna had been together a year. It was their anniversary tomorrow. In the jewellers, the young woman behind the counter asked him was the gold bracelet he was buying for his girlfriend.

"Yes," he replied quietly, his eyes darting around.

"She's a lucky girl." The woman said.

Geoff blushed and hurriedly shoved the carefully packaged gift into his pocket.

He hated Wednesdays because she took an extra art class and didn't get out of school until five pm. It was the only day of the week they didn't see each other. The only day of the week they didn't cycle home to her house together. The only day of the week he didn't follow her up to her bedroom to change out of her uniform. The only day of the week they didn't lie on her little single bed kissing and caressing. He really hated Wednesdays. And their anniversary was on a Wednesday.

He waited outside the school gates to surprise her.

It was early May and warm. He stood with his back to the wall, one foot flat against it. He was smoking a cigarette, the last one in the pack. He'd decided to give them up. Joanna hated him smoking and he knew it was stupid anyway - especially if he was becoming a doctor.

He'd tell her now that he was quitting smoking, he thought, as he stamped out the butt of his last Marlborough.

He opened a Wrigleys and began to chew on it - throwing the wrapper on the ground.

He pulled out his wallet to check that the gold bracelet was still there. And it was, wrapped in pink tissue paper - alongside a condom. 'Featherlight' it said on the unopened wrapper. He hurriedly moved the worn looking condom into the zipped part of his wallet.

He knew it was no good now anyway. Jimmy had grabbed his wallet from him that breaktime and taken out the condom, shouting "You've had this condom so long Geoff, it's bound to be dying of boredom."

Then he stuck a pin in it - over and over again. "I'm just putting it out of it's misery Geoff." So now the packet looked not only worn, but a bit like a teabag.

He looked at his watch. Five past five.

And sure enough. There she was. Cycling towards the gate - auburn hair blowing - no coat - socks around her ankles - jabbering as usual - to Kathy.

"Is that Geoff at the gate Joanna?"

They were cycling slowly.

She looked up and saw him. "Yes." She tried not to smile. Tried to hide how delighted she was to see him.

Kathy grinned knowingly at her. Encouraged, her face broke into a smile "It's our anniversary" she blurted.

Kathy speeded up and waved hello at Geoff as she passed by. Joanna stopped and stood, bike still between her legs. Hands on the handlebars.

"Hi."

"Hi." He kissed her awkwardly on the cheek. She was so small, he noticed for the umpteenth time.

He pulled out the pink tissue paper and handed it to her. "Happy anniversary" he said.

She opened it carefully, holding the bike upright with her legs.

"Oh Geoff - it's beautiful. Really beautiful." Her face felt as if it might break, she was smiling so much.

"I didn't think I'd see you today. I have your present - but it's at home. Will you come back with me?"

"OK, but I can't stay long - you know, study."

He threw his long leg over the saddle of her small racer and held it steady while she propped herself on the crossbar - one arm around his neck - the other on the middle of the handlebar, gripping it and her new bracelet so hard her hand hurt.

He cycled - knees sticking out as he pedalled. Legs brushing along hers.

There was a big hill approaching Joanna's house. You could see the sea from the top of it. They always pedalled hard going up then freewheeled down.

Just as they were coming to the brow of the hill he said in her ear, "I've quit smoking."

The bike was picking up momentum when she took her hand off the handlebar and put it along with her other one, around his neck and kissed him. She kissed him as his legs moved faster and faster with the pedals, as the wind blew harder, and as the little 5-gear racer wobbled all over the road. He kept his eyes open - and so did she - and they loved it.

It was a couple of weeks later when he asked her to

make love with him. He thought it was time. He noticed how she pushed herself towards him when they were in an embrace. How every muscle in his body became taut. She noticed it too. The peculiar feeling in the pit of her stomach and her heart beating faster and faster. And the feel of his flesh. She loved the feel of his skin. He had smooth skin, only his chest covered in dark curly hair. And he was so big. He wrapped himself around her. That made her feel so secure. And he touched her so carefully. She loved when he wasn't careful. When she knew he was feeling wild. With her. And she always wanted to touch him ... there. But never did. She could feel him through his jeans and through her jeans as she felt her own tightness and need to move.

And they moved together - just like on the dance floor. In time, in unison. She often wanted to put on music but was too shy to say it to him. So when he asked her - she said yes. Yes - she wanted to. And they did - one hot summer's day.

They were lying in her back garden with their friends. The phone rang. It was Joe, asking them all to go swimming in his back garden.They took one look at each other. Young, suntanned, ready. And said "No thanks Joe." Everyone else said "Yes."

They went upstairs to her room. She, in her bikini, he in his Speedos - wallet in hand. This time she did - touch him. It felt so foreign. She was terrified of hurting him. And he was even more terrified of hurting her. And so neither of them did.

It was their secret. He didn't tell Jimmy. She didn't tell Helen. Not for at least a month. They had a fight.

"It's all you're interested in, Geoff," she said to him, annoyed, as he stroked her leg one day toward the end of the summer. She didn't know why she said it as it was all she ever thought about too. Until recently. Recently she wanted ... What she wasn't sure.

It was that night after being in Kathy's that she told Helen. Helen seemed to understand what she meant.

"Oh Helen, I'm so glad you know what I mean," she looked at her earnestly. No fire.

"I really do ..."

"Oh my God - you and Jimmy?"

Helen had been going with him for a few months.

"Yes."

They both burst out laughing and hugged each other. Each really did know what the other meant.

* * *

Sixth year. Time for independence. For everybody - Joanna and Helen decided - at the same time - to finish with their boyfriends. Definitely. Little did they know that their boyfriends were thinking the same thing. They neither knew nor cared. They had been working part-time and had saved for a holiday - in France. Kathy was coming too. And they had no intention of being 'faithful' to their boyfriends, so they broke it off.

They spent night after night after night in Helen's house planning out their holiday, with help from Helen's father. He was able to tell them the cheapest way to do everything. Where to go - what to see.

And they were to start off and end at friends of his in Britanny. A beautiful village called Feins. They had a ball!

Four weeks away from home and they missed nobody. Boyfriends nor family. They found new boyfriends and didn't need their families. They learned to drink Pernod. Speak French. Pitch a tent. Deal with noisy train stations. Treat sunburn. And they came home tanned, 'sophisticated', inseparable and ready to conquer the world - or at least sixth year.

For months after they talked and laughed together about the holiday in that annoyingly exclusive way only seventeen year-old girls have.

"That reminds me of the night of the puncture" one of them would say raising her eyebrows.

The others would guffaw with laughter - not explaining the joke to anyone.

# Chapter Three

JOANNA MALONEY she scrawled across yet another document. She had never managed to develop a signature she liked and now she hated it.

Helen and her mother both beamed at her and they all hugged. The man across the table from them began to shuffle papers on the desk - tidying them into a file. He picked up a set of keys with a brown paper tag on them and handed them to Joanna.

"Well done," he shook her hand. "I hope it all goes well for you."

"Thanks Mr McGrath. I hope so too." She turned to the younger man beside her, shook his hand and kissed his cheek. "Thanks Tom. You've been fantastic."

Out on the street she and Helen said goodbye to her mother.

"Thanks Mum. I don't know what I'd have done without you. I'd probably have bought that place with the rising damp, dry rot, wet rot and ghosts and it would have fallen down around my ears within a week."

They all laughed.

"No, you wouldn't have Pet. I know you're sensible underneath it all." She looked at her watch. "I'd better get back to work fast. I said I'd only be an hour or so."

"OK, thanks Mum. See you tonight."

They ran to the car.

"She doesn't mean it you know," Joanna said as they got in.

"Mean what?"

"She doesn't think I'm sensible at all."

Helen rolled her eyes. "You take your mother for granted, you know that, don't you? She is about one hundred million times more liberal and more reasonable than any mother I know and you still manage to pick her up on everything."

"I do not!" Joanna replied, surprised at Helen's challenge.

"Yes you do. And anyway you're not."

"I'm not what?" Joanna asked, obviously annoyed.

"You're not sensible."

She took her eyes off the road to check her friend's expression. Helen was smiling, knowing exactly how to goad Joanna.

Joanna laughed. "You're a bad bitch Helen Ryan."

They pulled up directly outside the house.

It was detatched, small, quaint and wrecked. There was paintwork falling off everywhere. The garden was completely overgrown. The windows were cracked and there were slates missing off the roof. But Joanna thought it was beautiful. And Helen agreed.

"It's beautiful and it's going to be even more beautiful very soon."

They opened the gate with difficulty, and walked up to the door. It was old and heavy, but the lock was new and opened easily when Joanna turned the key in it. Then she fiddled with the keys for a moment and pressed one into Helen's hand.

"What's this?" Helen asked.

"It's the spare front door key. I want you to have it. I want you to be able to come and go - to consider this house a home - of sorts."

Later in O'Shea's, waiting for the gang to arrive, they clinked half pint glasses.

"It's unbelievable Joanna - really! Here you are, 22, with a great job, a car and now a house. It's quite incredible." Helen was shaking her head. "And here I am, 22, never had a job, living off the taxpayer with not a clue of what I'm doing, where I'm going next."

Joanna laughed. "Come on Helen, that's a load of crap, and you know it. You've done brilliantly in college. Managed to travel practically around the world each summer. And now finished top of the year in your MA. If that isn't successful, I don't know what is."

Helen grinned and took a noisy swig of her beer.

"You're absolutely right. We are the women of today. Young, successful, bright, gorgeous and happy."

It was true. They exuded an enviable self-assurance. In very different ways. Helen's outward, physical, obvious. Joanna's - more modest and less aware, but very apparent.

* * *

Joanna hadn't wanted to go to college. None of the subjects interested her. And anything that might have she didn't have the points for. Photography and painting were what she loved to do. So when she saw an ad in the paper looking for someone to work in a new video production company she didn't send in a CV but went to the address and asked to see the MD. Fortunately he was standing in reception and was amused by her directness. He talked to her for about an hour, then told her she had the job. It was badly paid and he made it clear to her that she'd have to work 'all hours' and 'at everything'. She was just eighteen.

There were only two others working there. A woman at reception, Jane, and a guy, Gerry, around her own age.

Derek was the boss. Still in his twenties and mad keen to make a go of his company. He smiled rarely, bit his nails and chain smoked.

There was a partner that Joanna heard little of.

"Suffice it to know he put a lot of money into the set-up of this little venture," Derek had told her on day one. He had smiled then.

The company grew, and Joanna along with it. She worked hard and it paid off. She, Gerry and Derek did everything themselves until after the first year, when they could afford to take on two more people full-time.

They found a graduate, Michael, who was more than handy with a camera. And then a first year student, Maire, who they felt would make a good Production Assistant.

It was Derek's responsibility to get the work in and keep the clients happy. Joanna's to decide, organise and oversee the shooting and editing - making sure they had a video at the end of it all. Maire worked to both Derek and Joanna, keeping them in line. Gerry did the editing. And Michael the camerawork.

It worked well. They became known and began to make money. Videos were becoming the rage. Everyone wanted a video - to promote their company, to record an event, to get onto the news, to train their staff.

They all worked weekends and nights without giving it a second thought. They ended up socialising together. It was always too late to call friends. And anyway they liked to talk shop and discuss problems over a drink in the evenings. They couldn't do that with their 'lay' friends.

"You're lucky you're already married." Gerry said to Derek as he was getting ready to leave on one of those evenings.

"Why?" said Derek.

"I don't get too much time to go out and meet new people, now do I Derek?"

Derek laughed. "No, I suppose you don't." He tossed Gerry's blond hair. "You'll be rich and famous soon and the women will be running after you then."

Joanna and Helen always tried to keep Saturday and Sunday nights free for each other, and their old friends.

* * *

Bbbrrring bbbrrring, bbbrrring bbbrrring, bbbrrring bbbrrring...

She opened her eyes. She was lying on her back. She glanced at the clock. A quarter to ten. It took her a moment to realise that she hadn't slept it out. It was Saturday morning and the phone was on its' fourth ring. She jumped out of bed and ran downstairs. "3427111," she said brightly as if she'd been awake for hours.

"I know that voice Joanna - you've literally just woken up and you're putting on your bright and breezy 'I never sleep in on a Saturday morning' voice."

"Jaysus Helen, I wouldn't exactly call this sleeping it in," she said smiling. "I don't understand you. You're always up so early at the weekends."

"I don't lead such a hectic life as you do my dear. I was trying to get a hold of you last night. I even had you paged in O'Shea's."

"Oh, you're not serious. It didn't even occur to me to call you. I thought you'd be wining and dining with your latest conquest."

She groaned.

"We went into town and went dancing - until three this morning."

"I have no sympathy for hangovers" said Helen "Get into the shower. Get dressed. Pack a bag with some clothes and a bikini and get over here rapid."

"Why? What are you talking about?"

"I'm talking about a sunny day and a free house. Mum and Dad have disappeared for the weekend and you and me are going to Brittas to get a suntan and then we're having a little party this evening."

Joanna was silent. She hadn't had a weekend off for weeks, possibly months. She looked out the window. It was sunny. She had a lot of work to do but it could wait until Monday. She could go in early.

"Joanna?"

"You're a genius. I'll be there soon." She hung up without saying goodbye.

"Mum?" She called as she took the stairs two at a time.

"Yes Pet." Her mother was already awake.

"That was Helen. Her parents are away and I'm going to stay with her for the weekend," she said as she walked into her mother's bedroom. The room that had been hers as a child. She had been moved out, into her parents' room a couple of months after her father left. At first she had hated it, feeling it wasn't her place. But then she got to like the space and the big double bed.

"No work this weekend?" her mother asked, surprised.

"Nothing that can't wait." She grinned. "If anyone's looking for me, give them Helen's number."

"Alright Pet, will you stick the kettle on when you go back down?" She went back to reading her book.

She crossed the landing to Rory and Conor's room. It was in semi-darkness and smelt musty. They never opened a window at night.

Rory's bed was empty - not unusual these days. The covers were pulled high over Conor's large form. He had grown tall, like their father. She sat on the end of the bed and grabbed his toes. He jerked his leg away, still not waking. She grabbed his other foot. He woke.

"Good morning Sleeping Beauty." She kissed him on the forehead. "Want some tea and toast? I'm making some for Mum."

He groaned at her.

"Of course you do." She swooshed open the curtains and went down to the kitchen leaving Conor to get accustomed to the bright morning light alone.

She brought her mother breakfast in bed. And she and Conor sat on high stools at the counter in the kitchen.

"Are you seeing Janine this weekend Con?"

"Yes." He smiled. A man of few words.

She began to pull clothes out of the 'to be ironed'

basket.

"I like her," she said.

"So do I!"

She laughed. "That helps of course." She picked up her bikini top and put it across her chest. "What do you think of this little number?"

"Divine - absolutely divine. Helen will look great in it."

"Rotten sod," she said and threw the top at him.

Helen opened the door before Joanna rang the bell.

"What kept you?" she asked, leaving the door open and dashing back inside. Joanna didn't bother answering. She couldn't be heard.

Helen came back grinning from ear to ear and looking ridiculous. Wearing a huge purple straw hat, purple shorts, a purple bikini top and a purple scarf. In one hand, a beach bag - the other, a freezer box.

"Let's go."

"You're going like that?" Joanna said.

"And why wouldn't I?" She ushered Joanna out of the house.

"Oh, no reason," she replied noticing the cool breeze on her own bare arms. "What's in here?" she asked as they put the freezer box into the boot.

"Just apples and champagne." Helen replied, extra casual.

"Apples and champagne!"

"Yes, apples and champagne."

Joanna opened the box and sure enough there were Granny Smiths and several bottles of 99p champagne cider. She roared laughing, throwing back her head. She always looked like she enjoyed her laugh.

"What's the occasion?" she asked getting behind the

wheel.

"Us." replied Helen "I'm taking a weekend off study and you're taking a weekend off work."

They smiled.

"Honestly Joanna, I thought you wouldn't be on for it, you know, I thought you'd be busy. You've been working so hard these days."

"Yes, I know. I was supposed to work this weekend but it really can wait. It must look like I'm obsessed with work. I'm not. It just takes all this effort to make a go of it. I'm still learning you know. Every day I come across yet another thing I don't know." She took her eyes off the road for a moment. "I haven't been neglecting you, have I Helen? I couldn't bear to be one of those women who drops all her friends because of the arrival of a man or whatever."

Helen was toying with Joanna's hair.

"A mere man is hardly likely to get in our way now is he?" She tugged a piece of hair gently. "You never neglect me Joanna. You sometimes neglect yourself and the rest of the world however." She studied Joanna's face. "You look wrecked these days Joanna. You need time off and some fun."

They spread out big beach towels and organised themselves for the day. They lay on their backs and rubbed in baby oil and only moved to get into the sea or to pop a bottle of champagne.

They got a little drunk and very sunburned and returned home laughing.

That night Kathy had to take over distributing the beer, answering the door and changing the records. Joanna and Helen couldn't move. Both had put on loose clothes and lathered on aftersun. They could still feel the heat of the sunburn through their clothes. Joanna's eyelids were so badly burnt that they'd swollen. If she tried to open them wide her skin felt as if it might break from the stretching. Every time they looked at one another they laughed, sorely, in solidarity and sympathy.

The gang left early - respecting their friends' discomfort.

They stripped off slowly and agonisingly in Helen's parents' bedroom.

Joanna put on a long cotton shirt and Helen couldn't bear to put on anything. They lay on top of the covers and left the windows open, letting the night air cool them.

As the sun rose they were still awake - talking in spurts.

"Feel my belly - it's like a furnace." Helen said as they were finally dropping off.

Joanna stretched across and gently laid her hand on Helen's stomach. She pulled her hand away suddenly.

"Christ it is." She began to laugh.

"What's so funny?"

"Us - look at the state of us. We're a couple of total idiots!"

* * *

Jane buzzed through to the edit suite.

"Joanna, sorry for disturbing you but Helen is on the phone - she says it's important."

"OK - thanks." She picked up the receiver and pressed the flashing button. Gerry turned down the sound and continued searching through footage for the next shot.

"Helen?"

"Joanna, I got it. I can't believe I got it. It's so incred..."

"Slow down," Joanna interrupted "got what?"

"The job. The job." Helen said excitedly.

"Which one - you've applied for loads."

"*The* job. The one in Hong Kong."

Joanna squealed "Oh my God Helen. That's fantastic. That's really fantastic. When do you go? For how long? How much? Oh we've got to celebrate. Oh no, I'll miss you so much."

A month later Joanna sat on Helen's bed watching her pack as she often had before for her many summers away.

"How on earth do you pack for a year?" Helen said in despair as she watched her huge suitcase filling to the brim and realised she had loads more things to put in it. Joanna pulled out two jumpers. "You're not going to need these are you?"

"I suppose not," she conceded.

"Great! I'll keep them safe for you until you get home."

"I'll need them when I come home for Christmas."

"Are you definitely coming home for Christmas?"

"I hope so. Sure we couldn't manage for an entire year without seeing each other."

After a couple of weeks Joanna got used to her not being around. They phoned each other about once a month and wrote often. Helen more often than Joanna. Joanna found it difficult to find the time to sit down and write. She never even got a chance to write in her jotters anymore.

## Chapter Four

Wa di, di, de, do, do, bum - beeeeeeeep. It's seven o'clock and this is the news read to you by Michael O'Neill.

"Morning Michael." She turned over and opened her eyes to check out the weather before she was told. "And the weather forecast today - scattered showers and outbreaks of rain." "Bullshit Michael, it's sunny where I am." She threw off her duvet, lay on her back for a moment, swung her legs off the bed and stood up. She walked to the radio and turned it up. "Beelzebub and the devil ..." she sang along with Freddie Mercury. Pulled on her tracksuit bottoms and sleeveless shirt - picked up her runners - winked at herself in the mirror and trotted downstairs. Counting in her head.

She switched on the immersion and the stereo.

"Sometimes wish I'd never been born at all, carry on, carry on" Freddie was singing as she laced up her runners and pushed her bike out the front door. "Nothing really matters to me." She closed Freddie and the door behind her, planting a big kiss on the shiny brass knocker.

"Back soon house."

She cycled along the seafront, moving up the gears, rarely sitting on the saddle. Just to the pier. Nodding greetings at the other regular early birds. The middle-aged skinny man who always wore a green vest with number nine on the front of it raised a hand when she passed. He always looked as if he was about to pass out. Then the grey haired sprightly woman walking her Jack Russell who always greeted her verbally. And last but not least, the attractive young man, with fair floppy hair, a great build and a great smile. He flicked his hair out of his eyes at Joanna every morning and smiled broadly. She smiled back. That was it - broad smiles. She was determined to talk to him - 'one of these days'.

There were other half-hearted regulars - one week on, one week off sort of thing. They didn't get the same friendly treatment as the conspiratorial four. She thought it would make a great name for an Enid Blyton book. *The Conspiratorial Four*.

Within fifteen minutes she was back - kettle on - shower. Cold fresh orange juice - hot buttered toast - tea - towel-dry hair in garden.

Bedroom - fresh faded jeans - white semi-button up shirt - cotton socks - sneakers. Keys, folder, sunglasses, bleep - into car - pull out onto clear road. Bidding farewell to her red door.

"Hi Derek" she shouted, walking into reception. "Want a cup of coffee?"

"Yes Joanna, please."

She made two cups of coffee, went in and sat opposite him in her favourite old leather swivel chair.

They discussed what work was coming up and the delegation of same. There were now eight of them working full-time in the company and they were taking on one more. They argued about the reshuffling of the existing staff, Derek promising to think about Joanna's suggestions.

They were doing fine. They had regular contracts and had recently landed a series of TV programmes with an American station: 'Irishy' half hours which Joanna had to edit in London and then personally deliver to New York. The eight programmes had gone well and Joanna was to finish them soon. She was tired of the toing and froing to London so she was glad.

But New York! She couldn't get enough of it. The first time she'd gone with Derek - just for two days. But the taste was enough. She was hooked.

The second time she was alone and stayed four days, walking the streets. Oblivious to the dangers of the neon-lit Times Square. In awe of the vastness of 5th Avenue. Charmed by Greenwich Village. Excited by Broadway. Horrified by Harlem. Addicted to Bloomingdales.

She'd been able to manage to decorate her house exactly as she'd wanted to. She and Helen had done it the first summer Helen was home. With a lot of help from her mother. She had bought a new car. Could afford great clothes. And had a terrific social life. Yet she always felt she wasn't doing enough. Felt that there was space in her brain for so much more. What, she asked herself often.

* * *

After work she met Fintan in the pub. He was already in the beer garden when she arrived. He stood, kissed her on the cheek and ordered her a drink without asking what she wanted - luckily getting it right.

They were 'dating' - sort of. He was warm, easy to be with and ... attractive? Yes, attractive. Tall, blond hair, blue eyes and a crinkly grin. He wore expensive casual clothes and worked in the bank. For some reason she always hated telling people that. But soon, he was going to Australia. He was taking voluntary redundancy. She thought it was a great idea and he didn't mind her lack of possessiveness. They knew they wouldn't keep in touch.

He spoke about his plans and she told funny stories about work. They charmed one another. And looked good together. She wondered how many other couples, sitting in the still warm sun in light shirts and dresses, looked suited and weren't.

A couple of drinks later they went their separate ways - to meet different friends. Without making any particular arrangement to meet again. He'd ring her 'at some stage' and that was fine.

She went home and changed. The phone rang as she was leaving the house.

"Hi gorgeous."

"Helen! Hi - It's wonderful to hear you. How are you doing?" she shouted.

"Fine - great - wonderful. And you?"

"About the same."

"Great. I'm coming home in less than a week."

"You're kidding. For how long?"

"The summer."

"Brilliant." Joanna was thrilled.

"And guess what? Laurent is coming with me for a few days. You'll meet him. Oh Joanna - I hope you'll like him."

"Of course I will - I'll love him. I know I will."

"Tell me about you, Joanna. You haven't written in ages. You're a terrible letter writer."

"No I'm not. I wrote only ..." She couldn't remember when.

"A month ago. And I've written twice since."

"I'm sorry Helen. I've been up to my eyes."

"Is Fintan still on the scene?"

"Sort of - not really. He's going off to Australia soon."

"Oh no Joanna, that's terrible."

"No it isn't. I think it's great - for him I mean."

"Not the man of your dreams so?"

"Definitely not. He's very sweet, but you know yourself." She laughed. "Listen though, Derek made me a shareholder and a director of the company a couple of weeks ago."

"That is fantastic. Omigod, I know someone rich and famous."

"Well, not quite yet."

"I'd better go Joanna - I'm going out to see Laurent now. We'll be over on Thursday week. I'll ring you the minute I get home."

"Great. I'm dying to see you."

"Me too. I miss you and miss you."

She felt warmed by the call. Helen had been in Hong Kong almost two years - but she had managed to get home twice and as ever Joanna was excited about seeing her friend. Indifferent about the boyfriend really. She doubted that he'd be good enough for Helen.

* * *

Saturday.

Dinner for four at Joanna's.

Helen, Laurent, Fintan and Joanna.

She was annoyed at herself about the fuss she was making about the food - simply because Laurent was French. She had even phoned her mother for advice. And she had bought very expensive white wine - not knowing if it was good or not.

Helen's letters to Joanna were frequent, happy and intimate as ever. She felt life couldn't get any better. She and Laurent, who was a lecturer in the same university, were talking about moving in with each other when they went back after the summer.

Joanna was dying to see Helen. She had been in London editing a rush job on Thursday when Helen had flown in. She phoned her from her hotel in London to arrange the evening.

Promptly at eight the doorbell rang. Joanna ran to open it. Fintan followed her to the door. Smiling faces. Hers and theirs.

She was amazed at how similar Helen and Laurent looked. He was sallow, dark-eyed and dark-haired - silky, floppy hair like Helen's.

Joanna and Helen threw their arms around each other and hugged for a few moments, leaving the men smiling awkwardly in the background. Laurent kissed

Joanna's cheeks - four times - while shaking her hand. He had a good handshake. Helen in the meantime was doing the same with Fintan, who was embarassed by all this open show of affection.

Joanna ticked herself off for thinking 'Jaysus, we're not French.' And then again for criticising Fintan to herself for assuming the male role of drink pouring. 'Joanna, you are never happy,' she muttered to herself as they all settled in.

She had thought it might be a tough evening - and it was. Laurent talked mostly to Joanna, anxious to impress his woman's best friend. He'd 'heard so much about her'. Joanna felt a bit uncomfortable with him. He looked unblinkingly at the person he was talking to, and he touched often. Laying a hand on Joanna's arm or turning to kiss Helen's cheek. Joanna found herself searching for Fintan's less intense, more relaxed eyes. And smiled gratefully at them when found. Helen watched Joanna and Laurent carefully - making sure they were getting along and clearly finding it difficult to divide her attentions. One minute completely engrossed with Joanna. The next Laurent. And then Fintan - politely - almost as an afterthought. She was having difficulty dividing her physical attentions too. Flitting around like a butterfly resting her hand on Laurent's shoulder and then Joanna's, sometimes actually touching them both simultaneously.

Joanna was aware of it all and felt edgy. She knew how important it was for her to like Laurent - he was 'the man'. There had never been anyone there before to challenge their friendship.

He was perfectly spoken, perfectly mannered, perfectly dressed. She couldn't and wouldn't fault him.

She just wished he wouldn't stare at her like that.

Thankfully it wasn't a late evening. Laurent was flying home to Paris in the morning. Fintan raised his eyebrows at Joanna across the table as they were leaving. She looked back and nodded at him - wanting him to stay the night, appreciating his non-assumption and simply his presence. Helen noticed the exchange and looked away.

The next morning Joanna found an excited Helen on her doorstep.

"What did you think of him?"

"I think he's absolutely gorgeous - wonderful - fantastic." She laughed. "Pour yourself a cup of coffee - it's fresh - and come upstairs, I'm still in bed. Fintan's in the shower."

"Oh." Helen looked unsure. "I'm sorry Joanna. Do you want me to come back later? I should have called - I didn't think. I just came straight here from seeing off Laurent."

"Oh for God's sake Helen, don't be ridiculous. Get that cup of coffe and come on upstairs."

While Helen was in the kitchen, Joanna picked up Fintan's clothes and brought them into him in the bathroom. When she went back to her room Helen was sitting on the end of the bed.

"You *really* like Laurent?" she asked in a semi-whisper as Joanna got back under the covers.

"Yes, I really like Laurent. I think he's great!" She wanted to say words like 'special', 'interesting', 'unusual', but couldn't because she didn't think so.

"I'm so relieved Joanna. I don't know why it's so important to me but it is." She looked at her shyly.

"You have to like him - one of the reasons I love him is because he's so much like you."

"Like me?" Joanna was surprised "How?"

"Oh, he's generous and impulsive and bright and funny - he really is like you."

Just then Fintan walked into the room, fully dressed, his hair still wet. Joanna found herself admiring his appearance, as she often did, in a detatched, distant sort of way. And she wondered, yet again, what it was he was attracted to in her, assuming always it was her lack of possession and her independence - ignoring her own physical attractiveness.

He smiled at Helen. "Good to see you again Helen." He looked to Joanna. "I'm off to the match Joanna, I'll give you a call soon."

Joanna moved to get out of bed.

"Don't get up - I'll see myself out."

She smiled at him and was glad he didn't kiss her like he usually did when leaving.

"What sport does he play?" Helen asked when she heard the front door bang closed.

"None - he's going to watch a soccer match."

"Oh!" There was silence for a moment. "He's terrific Joanna," Helen said without meeting her eyes. Joanna knew it was a token comment and there was a huge unspoken 'but' at the end of it. She was amused and said nothing.

Helen suddenly kicked off her shoes and got into the bed beside Joanna. The action threw them back to their old selves and happily, they left the talk of men behind and went on to talk about plans for the summer and for their futures.

Helen and Laurent were both due back in Hong Kong at the beginning of September. But for the next three months they were going to have fun. Joanna would take as much time off work as possible. She was glad that Fintan was going away soon.

* * *

They sat in the darkness - assessing the movie - silently. The screen now blank. They were sitting, half leaning on each other on the bed. Both a little woozy from the wine - and relaxed by one another's company. Comfortable - an inadequate word, but accurate.

"Well, what did you think of it?" Helen broke the silence first.

"It was quite good, I suppose."

"You just think that because you love Mel Gibson."

Joanna whisper-laughed. "You're right as usual."

"Admit it, it was corny, badly made and B-rated."

"OK, OK it was."

This summer they were spending more time together than ever before. Calling each other a couple of times a day and spending each evening together. A day didn't feel complete if they didn't see each other. They often commented on their friendship and how unalike they were in terms of lifestyle, yet how close.

They were both thinking about this now.

The video screen had gone snowy, casting a little distorted light onto their faces. Joanna put her glass on the bookshelf. She said nothing - didn't want to break the silence. Helen leaned over her and did the same. Moving back to her position she brushed Joanna's cheek with her lips. They stared at each other for what seemed like minutes, neither knowing what to do next. Well, both knowing but each afraid to make the move. Their timing as usual matched as they moved toward each other. Kissed lips, cheeks, lips again. So softly they could have been butterfly kisses. Then they stroked each other's lips with their tongues and caressed their faces with their hands - no more. Soon, they sat back from each other. Everything felt like slow motion. Neither spoke.

In one long slow movement they stretched out on the bed. Joanna half lying on Helen.

"Helen?"

"Yes?"

"Why are we doing this?"

"Because", she pushed Joanna's hair back off her face "we want to." They kissed again. Already getting used to the feeling of softer, gentler lips.

# Chapter Five

It grew. Whatever it was - it grew.

In the following weeks they spent every free moment they had with each other. They were a bit unsure at times. Not knowing if it was OK to touch the other. Not wanting to invade privacy. At the same time not able to stop.

They decided to go to Donegal for a few days. To the house that Joanna had gone to as a child. She organised for someone to take on her work and for Conor to look after her house and off they went.

"I've always loved going on long car journeys with you."

"Me too," Joanna replied, turning over Carly Simon. Then she slipped her hand under Helen's thigh and left it there - palm resting on the driver's seat. Helen flexed her thigh, acknowledging the presence of her new-found lover's hand - which remained there until they switched seats, just before the border. Then Helen's hand rested in the exact same spot.

They talked - for five solid hours. About what was happening to them. About childhood holidays. Whoever was passenger chose the music. It never mattered to the other. Their taste in music matched. Leonard Cohen, Chariots of Fire, Carol King. Sometimes they wouldn't notice a tape playing twice, even three times.

It was a big, three-storeyed house, overlooking the sea. The front door had been left open, awaiting their arrival. A set of keys and a note lay on the old pine table in the kitchen. They ran around the house checking out the rooms. Joanna testing her memory before entering each room.

Helen stood in a doorway and said "Let's take this one."

Joanna stood on the opposite side of the corridor saying "Well, I think we should take this one," knowing what was behind the door. "But, you can sleep over there if you want" she grinned, turned, went into her room and closed the door.

There was a tap on the door.

"Enter."

Helen came in and burst out laughing. "Yeah, sure" she said nodding at the single bed and baby cot. Before they had left for Donegal they had talked shyly about the freedom of being in a house, a place they weren't known. Not having to worry about their family or friends 'noticing'. Being free to touch each other in the way they'd just discovered. They talked about sex, but in a general way - not directly about what they were doing. What was happening them.

They didn't talk yet about lesbianism or heterosexuality. They savoured their time together and marvelled at themselves - often.

"Can I have a hug?" They were still so uncertain.

Joanna smiled and hugged her tight. "You can always have a hug."

They went into the room Helen had chosen.

"My parents used to sleep here." Joanna said.

"Would you prefer we used another room?"

"No, I always loved it."

It was on the top floor, had a big double bed and a sloping ceiling. A huge square window overlooked the sea. 'The Lagoon' was what they called the cove surrounded by rocks.

That night they sat in front of the fire reading and listening to the old radio - one like you'd see on The Waltons. Helen preferred plays and chat shows - Joanna liked music. That night neither of them cared. They sat, leaning against one another on the couch. Full after their dinner. Tired after their long journey.

They went to bed quietly, almost nervously. Donned nightshirts and switched off the centre light. There were no lamps.

As soon as they were under the covers they turned to face each other. Joanna's hand rested on Helen's cheek. She didn't speak until she found her night eyes.

"You know Helen, I feel completely safe - here - with you."

Helen smiled.

"I mean normally, in a place like this I'd be a bit scared. I always was when I was younger. You know, scared of the dark. Of noises. Oh of everything. *You* know."

Helen smiled gently - that smile when she didn't open her lips - a smile kept for special people. And kissed her.

They moved closer, moulding into each other. Legs entwining - hands touching skin. Smooth, young, warm skin. They took off their nightshirts so they could feel skin on skin.

Joanna thought Helen was beautiful but was too shy to say it. She kissed her neck - drew her tongue from her lips to her breasts. Brushing each one lightly with her lips - then taking a nipple in her mouth - sucking it - drawing on it gently. Helen's breath caught. She arched back, pushing herself further into Joanna's mouth. She held her hair back from her face - so she could watch. Joanna looked back at her. She kissed across to her other breast, eyes still locked. When mouth found nipple - Helen's eyes closed momentarily. "If only you could see yourself. It looks so beautiful," she whispered when she re-opened her eyes.

Much, much later they fell asleep. Still entwined. Warm, safe, undisturbed sleep.

They woke in the morning to sunshine and knocking on the front door. Joanna jumped out of bed immediately, grabbed her robe and ran downstairs.There was a smiling, young-looking elderly woman there.

"Hello Mrs O'Reilly," she said as she opened the door.

"Joanna, dear, how are you? And the family? How're your parents?"

"Great thanks - everyone is great," she replied, it always being easier - less embarrassing to mention her father at all.

"And you dear - you haven't changed a bit."

Joanna smiled "Nor have you". She had always liked Mrs O'Reilly.

Mrs O'Reilly preened visibly.

"Well I can't complain. I can't complain. Now is everything alright for you - do you need anything?"

"No - everything is perfect."

"I see just one car," she looked towards the car in front of the house. "There aren't many of you here?"

"No, just myself and my ..." she hesitated for a moment, wondering to herself what was Helen now, "friend."

The smile dropped away from the woman's face, aging her five years immediately. Joanna realised what she thought.

"A quiet weekend so," she said coldly. But then a smile re-appeared as she looked over Joanna's shoulder, "Oh, is *this* your friend?"

Joanna turned to a bleary-eyed Helen, barely able to hold her laugh in.

"Helen. This is Mrs O'Reilly, who owns the house."

"Hello, Mrs O'Reilly. It's a lovely house - lovely place."

"Oh yes dear it is, isn't it." Smiling broadly now. "I just called in to welcome you, and to update Joanna here on the local ... scene." She liked the fact she could be so 'with it' for these young Dubliners. "There's a new Spar shop in the town Joanna. It's the best place for food. They have a meat counter ... and a wine licence."

"That's great." In unison.

"And I'm sure you'll be looking for a little nightlife too" she laughed a little - all girls together now.

Helen and Joanna exchanged glances.

"The Hotel is the only place to go really. Well, the only *decent* place - the boys won't know their luck. Two lovely girls like you in town for the weekend." She looked from one to the other. 'Girls together' laughed.

"Thanks a million Mrs O'Reilly - that's a great help."

"I'll be off so. If you need anything, you know where I am."

She left, still smiling.

Joanna closed the door behind her and waved. She fell against the door, laughing, scrunching her face against the clear glass - cooling her hot cheeks.

"The boys won't know their luck." Helen mimicked behind her.

"Oh God Helen, you should have seen her face when she thought I was here with a man - *out of wedlock* - aah!" Her breath was fogging up the window.

"I'd love to see her face if she saw this." Helen whispered as she pressed into Joanna's back, putting her hands on her breasts.

Joanna literally jumped. "Jesus Helen - be careful."

Helen put her hands on her shoulders and turned her around sharply. "I am not ashamed of this."

"Nor am I." Joanna brushed by her. "I'm just not used to it."

They spent the day alone. Exploring the lagoon. Swimming in almost warm water - the sand had all morning to heat up before the water washed in around the outer rocks - although beyond the lagoon the sea was choppy, cold, daunting.

They lay on towels. Silent. Engrossed in thoughts - of one another.

"What are you thinking about?" Joanna asked when she noticed Helen looking at her for some time.

"You - you're so pretty."

"I'm not - I'm horrible."

She grabbed Joanna's hand. "Don't ever say that - please. You're lovely. *You're lovely*. You have one of the prettiest faces I've ever seen. And your hair," she stroked it "your hair is beautiful."

Joanna put the palm of Helen's hand to her mouth.

"Thank you" she whispered into it.

They decided to give the boys in town a thrill that night. Joanna showered, washed her hair, put on fresh faded jeans, white runners and a brilliant white sweatshirt. While Helen got ready she went out to the rocks of the lagoon and stood in the wind drying her hair.

Helen watched her from their bedroom window. Her auburn hair, caught by sunlight, blowing wildly around her white sweatshirt. "My woman," she said aloud as she watched Joanna clamber easily over the rocks - leaping and laughing and shaking her head.She had never seen her friend look so happy. Ever. And for some reason she wanted to cry but didn't quite know why.

Joanna was remembering, with pleasure, how she used to pride herself at being 'as good a rock climber' as her brothers. Always pushing herself that little bit further. Always making that longer jump. And they, encouraging her, not helping - she'd never let them help.

There was one jump she could never make. It was a gully. Narrow enough, but high above the sea. She had always been afraid of it.

But "I'm 24, and taller now - and afraid of nothing" she thought to herself as she ran at it with certainty.

She jumped, only looking at the other side. And landed, her runners gripping the dry, sloping rock surely. She threw herself forward on all fours. Then stood with her arms up in the air, yelling, waving and turning. As if she was an Olympic gold medallist with a massive audience.

Heads turned when they walked into the hotel bar. Possibly because they were the only women. Possibly because they were glowing.

They sat at the bar - very close - facing each other - legs interlocked. Joanna had never been so aware of another person's touch before. They touched for every posssible excuse - to show each other something - to restrain - to express just about anything - simply to get physically closer. And when one of them went to the loo, the other waited impatiently feeling almost bereft, until they saw the swing of the toilet door and the smile of their lover. Then they'd settle again - entwining some part of their bodies.

There was a dart match going on. Three young men were playing. Swaggering past Helen and Joanna to pull the darts out of the board. Trying to impress their peers and potential conquests with their precision and nonchalance.

But the two young women were completely unaware

of the attention being lavished on them. Heads bowed - glasses cupped. They were talking about Joanna's father, as they did sometimes. Helen always wanting to understand what it must be like to lose your father so early in life.

"No - it's so much not like he's dead. I mean every day I wonder about him. Wonder where he is. What he's doing."

"But would you like to see him?" Helen asked. Joanna thought for a moment.

"I'd love to see him. I'd be scared I think. But yes. I would." She bent her head. "I really love him you know." The hand that was on her arm began to stroke it.

"I remember so many things about him. Good things. Sometimes I pretend I don't - it's easier that way." She was silent. "Do you know what I mean Helen?"

"I think so."

Joanna looked at her "It's a stupid question really."

"What is?"

"Do you know what I mean?" She smiled. "You always know what I mean."

Just then, one of the young men - tired of hitting double tops unnoticed, tapped Joanna's shoulder, "Could we buy you girls a drink?"

He had a nice smile - and a gorgeous soft Donegal accent. They spent the rest of the evening flirting, drinking and playing darts. And left unfulfilled but hopeful faces behind with promises of 'tomorrow night'.

Slightly merry, they sang along with Aretha Franklin in the car. "R.E.S.P.E.C.T" Joanna wailed, her finger dancing on the steering wheel. Helen's passenger seat jive couldn't be outdone.

Helen was already in bed when Joanna came into the room - mouth cold with toothpaste. She undressed hurriedly.

"Don't," said Helen almost sharply when she reached for her nightshirt.

She pulled the bedclothes down around her waist. She was naked.

Joanna said nothing. She reached for the light switch.

"Don't" came again.

Joanna stood, still in her knickers, looking at her. She was rooted - immobile.

"Come to bed."

"I can't," she eventually replied and thought 'Where are the seagulls and the howling wind when you want them?' as the silence grew.

"I have to switch the light off," she said desperately. "I ... You know how I am about - my body." She was holding her arms protectively across her breasts.

"What are you talking about. You're lovely. And this is me." Helen replied incredulously. "I *want* to see you - to look at you."

Joanna's head was bent. She was looking at the ground - near to tears.

"Helen, I just can't." Her voice broke.

Helen jumped out of the bed and took her in her arms, "Don't be upset - I'm sorry - I didn't realise," she said gently, switching off the light. "You're freezing - get into bed." She pulled the covers up over her and went to the window. She pulled open the curtains. "Is that OK, Joanna?"

"Yes."

"Are you sure?"

"It's perfect."

She was sitting up, covers around her shoulders. They could see the moon - a full moon - its reflection shimmering across the still water in the lagoon. They watched it for a while. Both in private thoughts.

Helen was amazed at all she still didn't know about her friend after so long, and wanted now to discover everything about her.

And Joanna thought too of what Helen didn't know and was surprised at herself for being able to tell her some of her deepest fears. She looked from the moon to Helen, leaning against the window frame. Her sallow skin paled by the moonlight. Oblivious of her own nakedness.

"Joanna?"

"Yes?"

"When did you know?"

"About this?" Joanna asked.

"Yes."

"I didn't." Joanna smiled. "I didn't know at all."

"You mean literally until the night we kissed?"

"I think so. It's so hard to say." Joanna thought for a moment before going on. "I know we'd both talked about this sort of thing in an abstract way but if I ever really tried to think about it I couldn't. Do you know what I mean?"

"Yes - I feel pretty much the same." Helen replied. "Do you think you're a lesbian?"

Joanna laughed. "I believe that's what this is called my dear."

"Seriously Joanna."

"Oh, I don't know Helen. I mean what we are doing is called lesbianism. So if that makes me a lesbian then I'm a lesbian."

"But you like men." Helen persisted.

"I have liked men. Yes."

"So if someone asked you were you homosexual or heterosexual what would you say"?

"I'd say it was none of their business."

Helen smiled "Yes, but then what would you say?"

"I suppose I'd say 'I'm sexual - why the need to give me a label?' and then I'd say 'and it's still none of your business.'"

Helen moved from her place by the window and got into bed, immediately wrapping her arms around Joanna. No shyness. She kissed her. "Imagine going through life and never discovering this?" she said as they kissed.

That night their lovemaking was passionate in a way neither of them knew woman and woman could be.

They kissed and touched for hours. Discovering what pleased the other. *Knowing* what pleased the other. It was easy. Their bodies matched so perfectly. Soft on soft. Smooth on smooth.

"I feel like a virgin." Helen whispered.

"So do I."

And that night they made each other come - for the first time. They watched each other come - for the first time. They lay naked, side by side in the moonlight - the covers kicked down to the end of the bed - body heat still warm enough. They were looking at each other - not speaking. And that's how they fell asleep.

About an hour later Joanna woke - shivering. She reached down and pulled the covers over both of them. Helen was in a deep sleep.

It was already getting bright. There was a hint of the moon still there. She smiled at it - kissed Helen's bare shoulder and snuggled down to sleep.

But sleep would not come. Her mind was racing. She was thinking - about Helen. About how much she loved her. How safe she felt with her. How much fun they had. How happy they were with one another. But now she felt uneasy, agitated and she tossed and turned. She decided to go out for a walk. Silently she dressed in jumper, jeans and runners and crept out of the room, leaving the door ajar.

Slowly, she walked around the lagoon and onto the outer rocks, to the one she'd named her own as a child. It was a beautiful morning. The sea was so calm within the lagoon - even outside it. It was like looking at someone asleep - its swell, just a gentle breath. The dawn chorus sang in her ears. She always thought it was the most beautiful orchestra in the world. An orange semi-circle was flaming on the horizon. Rising rapidly. She searched for the moon but it had gone. And sitting there she began to sob quietly - into her knees. Suddenly she threw her head back and cried out. "Let this be - please let this be," her voice lost on the sleeping sea.

Helen didn't wake. Didn't notice Joanna's absence until she returned.

"You're freezing" she said when Joanna got into bed, still in her sweatshirt. "Where have you been?"

"Just for a walk."

Helen drew her breath in sharply when she put her warm feet on Joanna's cold - she hated cold things. She reached under Joanna's sweatshirt and fell asleep only after she'd rubbed her warm again.

They got up late that day - showered and prepared a big cold salad for brunch. Nutty brown bread, ham, cheese, apples and orange juice.

They ate outside - the sun already high in the sky - and hot.

"Helen?"

"Yep?"

"When are you going back?" she asked, keeping her eyes closed, face turned to the sun.

"I'm supposed to be going back in a month. But I've been thinking about that ... and, well, I thought maybe I'd stay right up until term starts - which would mean I'd have seven more weeks altogether." She took Joanna's hand "What do you think? I mean, I won't stay if you don't want me to."

"Of course I want you to - of course I do." She was looking at her now. "But Helen, what about Laurent? I don't want ... this - us" she squeezed her hand "to come between the two of you."

Helen looked away.

"It won't. He'll understand. He knows how important ... home is to me."

"But won't you miss him?" she persisted.

"Maybe - I don't know. I know I don't ever miss him when you and I are together." She laughed. "And anyway I've my whole bloody life to spend with him don't I?"

Joanna closed her eyes and leaned back, pretending to sunbathe. The sun felt too hot, making her want to rub and ease her skin. She didn't want Helen to see her tears.

Later, while Helen was showering she began her nineteenth jotter.

*I'm not too sure what's going on here. Not too sure at*

*all. I know I've always thought this sort of thing fine. But is it for me? It feels so right. How can it not be for me? She seems to feel it's right too. So that's fine. But where does it go from here? It can't go anywhere really, can it?*
*Be careful woman, be careful!*

# Chapter Six

And then, and then, and then, oh God, and then.

They decided to stay a couple of extra days. Joanna called her office. Helen called home. Everyone was happy. Except the local men. They were disappointed. The gorgeous women stayed home. They stayed home and loved each other.

The following morning Helen woke first - unusually. She went downstairs and got two glasses of juice. Joanna was still sleeping when she returned to the room. She sat on the edge of the bed looking at her - content - undisturbed. She laid her hand on Joanna's cheek. Joanna began to wake.

"Morning - how are you?"

"Fine," she replied through sleepy eyes.

Helen bent suddenly and held her lips against her cheek. "Joanna, I love you. I love you and - and so much more. Do you know what I mean?" she said almost desperately.

Joanna opened her eyes.

"Just, and and and - I love you -and and and."

"Yes, that's what I mean. I love you, and and and."

Joanna never thought the words 'I love you' could be so inadequate. But suddenly, that day, they were. 'I love you' did not describe the emotions each felt for the other. Somehow 'and and and' did a better job of it.

Midweek, the weather broke. Joanna had been off work too long and Helen's parents were getting agitated. They went home - to Dublin - in love. Except for that one time they never talked of Helen's return to Hong Kong - or of her lover who would be waiting patiently for her. Joanna felt like a patient in remission. Two whole months until mid-September.

They went out to dinner or the theatre or the pictures every other night - alone, and in general behaved like lovers. Always returning home, not too late, to make love. For the most part it went unnoticed. Except in Joanna's work - and in Helen's home.

Her parents discussed her reasons for changing her flight back to Hong Kong.

"I presume she's having problems with that fella of hers," her father commented.

"I don't know" her mother said. "There seems to be more to it than that. She seems terribly happy here, you know, off this place and that all the time, really enjoying herself." Her eyes widened and she spoke her thought aloud. "Goodness, maybe she's thinking of coming home for good."

* * *

Derek called Joanna into the office.

"You're always rushing off these days Joanna. Come on in for a chat."

Joanna sat in her favourite swivel chair and spun around.

"How's the edit going?" He fidgeted with one of those executive toys - the one with the silver clanking balls.

"You tell me Derek - you saw it this morning." She smiled, reaching over to stop the balls clanking. He picked up a Marlborough and offered her one. He always forgot she didn't smoke.

"It's shaping up well I think - hard to tell yet."

"It'll be good, don't worry."

"I'm not."

He took a long drag on his cigarette. "You seem a bit ... distracted these days. I mean you run out of here the minute the machines are turned off and ..."

"Is my work less than par?" Joanna interrupted, bristling.

"Oh God no - the opposite - you seem to be racing through huge amounts of work, and it's all good." He took another drag. "It's just you. I feel you're on another planet when you're not working. I mean, you never come in here any more. We hardly talk, except at official meetings. Is there something wrong - with here - with me?"

It was her turn to say "Oh no, definitely not."

"I'm going to be straight with you Joanna, and you can tell me to piss off if you like." He set the balls in action and looked at her. "Are you being poached? Are you moving?"

She burst out laughing, walked over to him, put her hand on the swinging balls and kissed him on his receding hairline.

"No Derek - I'm not being poached - you flatter me. Pity though. I could force you to give me more money, and if you put your hand on those balls once more I *will* leave."

He laughed.

"I'm not being poached - I am, however, in love."

He looked at her, amazed. "You're kidding!"

She pucked him on the shoulder. "Don't look so bloody surprised. It does happen you know."

"I'm sorry. It's just that you never seem to take us poor male mortals seriously - that's all."

She laughed again. This time giving no explanation. And left.

She had never said those words aloud, not even to Helen. She had said she loved her hundreds of times, but they used to say that even before they were lovers.

Helen was pulling up outside the house as she was putting the key in the door.

"I wasn't sure when you'd get home," Helen called. "I stopped off at the supermarket on my way." She held up two shopping bags, ran up to her and kissed her on the lips.

Joanna told her about the conversation with Derek and they laughed.

"I'm glad nobody knows - aren't you?"

"I suppose I am really," Joanna replied. "Why though - why are you?"

"Oh I don't know - nothing to do with ... lesbianism or anything - I don't give a damn about that. It's just -

our business." She looked up. "If no one knows - no one can interfere." She smiled.

"Helen?"

"Yes?"

"I am in love with you. You know that don't you?"

Helen put her hands to the back of Joanna's head and kissed her. "I certainly hope so my love. I don't think I could bear being so much in love with someone who wasn't in love with me."

Later that night, just as they were going asleep, Helen stroked Joanna's hair and whispered,

*"Good friend, you are my only friend*
*You think the same of me*
*You swear our love will always last*
*Though lapped in secrecy*
*Like all true love should be."*

Joanna's eyes flew open "Where did you hear that?"

"It's a poem by Robert Graves." She turned her back to Joanna so she could snuggle into her and rest her hand on her stomach - the way they always slept now.

"*Like all true love should be,*" she repeated before they fell asleep.

The next day was Saturday. They slept late. Joanna waking first. She was always impatient for Helen to wake but never woke her. But this morning was different.

"Get up, get up, get up, you lazy donkey,
Get up, get up, get up you sleepy head,
Get up, get up, get up you lazy donkey,
You lazy donkey get out of bed."

Helen couldn't but wake.

"I used to sing that when I was a kid."

"Oh God no" Helen groaned, "You're not in one of your lively humours, are you?"

"You're damn right I am."

She slid out of bed and quickly pulled on a long shirt. "Time for orange juice aaannnnnnnnnd guess what?"

"What?" came muffled from under the duvet.

"*The Waltons.*"

Helen sat bolt upright "*I* am not watching *The Waltons.*"

"Oh yes you are my dear - ten thirty - Channel Four. And if you misbehave I'll record it - tie you to the bed and make you watch it all day." She was in the kitchen pouring out fresh orange juice.

Helen followed her - she was naked.

"You can tie me down - I won't resist - In fact I might even encourage it. You can do what you like with me - but I refuse to watch *The Waltons.*"

"Sorry. No choice. I always watch *The Waltons* on a Saturday morning."

"But that doesn't mean I have to, now does it?" asked Helen, drinking her juice.

"Of course it does - and please, put on some clothing - I live in a respectable neighbourhood," said Joanna as she walked into the bedroom, switched on the TV and sat up on the bed - remote in hand. She sang along with the sig tune loudly.

Helen stood - hands on hips - in front of the TV.

"This town ain't big enough for both of us - and it ain't me who's going to leave," she sang as she switched off the TV, jumped on top of Joanna and pinned her arms above her head kissing her manically.

"I wanna watch *The Waltons.*"

Helen kissed her more slowly "You wanna what?"

"Watch *The Waltons*," Joanna whispered.

Helen kissed her once more, this time holding both Joanna's arms with one of her own and caressing her with her free hand. "You wanna what?"

Joanna replied with a long deep kiss.

When Helen began to take off her shirt she held her wrists. "Don't".

"Am I hurting you?" Helen asked, lifting herself up on her arms.

"No," Joanna smiled, "I just don't want to take off my shirt."

"Why?" Helen asked - Joanna looked around the room and said nothing.

"Oh, oh - daylight strikes again."

Joanna smiled and nodded.

"Oh you idiot - I love your body - every inch of it."

Joanna made a face.

"Oh, oh - but you don't."

She nodded.

"My silly little love," Helen said as she bent her head and kissed her through the cotton.

She rolled Joanna over - on top of her - and drew her finger hard along the length of her spine.

"That feels so good."

Helen rolled her over again. This time lying on her back in between Joanna's legs, her head lying between her breasts, still kissing each other.

"Touch me Joanna."

Joanna caressed her breasts, over her shoulders.

Suddenly she couldn't bear the cotton barrier any more and pulled off her shirt.

"That's better," Helen said as she turned to look at her.

Later - after they'd showered - Joanna said "You're so

free with your body - It's great. I envy you."

Helen kissed her on the forehead "You'll get there Pet -don't worry."

* * *

Saturday.

Shopping and family day in middle class suburbia. In the supermarket she remembered to buy spicy things and cheese for Helen, plain food for herself. When she got home - home home - Conor was poring over photos and details from auctioneers. He was getting married soon and was house-hunting.

"Joanna, will you give us a hand filling out the loan application for the Building Society?"

"Sure. Are you definitely going with the Building Society?"

"That's where our savings are - where else could we go?"

"I got mine from the bank - it's a bit more expensive though." She was chewing on a piece of bread and ham."Wow Conor, I love this one - have you seen it yet?" She pointed to an old single-storey cottage with a huge garden.

"Not yet. We're seeing it today."

"Where's Mum?"

"In town - she'll be home soon. She's buying a birthday present to send over to Rory."

"Oh Christ, I forgot his birthday was coming up."

"I wouldn't worry about it - no one has heard from him in months."

"You'd think he was in bloody Australia - not London - what the hell is he doing now anyway?"

"Not much the last I heard."

Joanna picked up the family photo that sat under the clock. "He was so different when he was younger - he's the image of our father."

"You say that every time you look at that photo."

She laughed and put it down. "I'm envious - I didn't get the good looks."

The phone rang."It's Kathy for you," Conor called.

"Kathy - Hi," she was genuinely pleased to hear from her friend.

"Well where the hell have you been? I've been trying to contact you for over a week."

"Oh - I'm sorry. We were away for a few days."

"We - we - who's we? Is there some new man I don't know about?"

Joanna laughed "Don't be ridiculous - just Helen and myself."

"Oh you two - the inseparables. Enough of this idle banter - party time tonight - my place after O'Shea's, OK?"

"Great."

"Yourself and Helen and any poor unfortunate males you feel like putting your hands on."

After they'd hung up she rang Helen at her parents' house to tell her.

"My parents are going away for a long weekend next weekend. They really want me to go - say they haven't seen me at all. Will you come too Joanna?"

"Oh Helen, I can't - I've a shoot next Saturday."

"Fuck it - you're kidding?"

"I'm not - fuck it is right - how long?"

"Five days"

"Jesus - five days - that's ages."

"I know - damn, damn, damn."

Silence for a moment.

"I'm going to have dinner with Mum and Conor. I'll see you in the pub later, OK?"

"Perfect - I'm doing the same.

"Bye so."

"Joanna? - I love you."

Later, Joanna and her Mother went for a walk along the strand with Simba - their old black labrador. The tide was full in and the water was as grey as the sky.

"I hope the weather isn't breaking - it's been so wonderful" her mother said - disturbing the familiar silence between them. Joanna barely heard her.

"You're miles away Joanna - is there anything bothering you?"

"God no Mum. Things couldn't be better - really," she assured her.

"How's work?"

"Fine - I'm taking it easy though - just while Helen's home."

"That's a good idea. You were working such long hours, I was a bit worried about you. Helen will be off soon I suppose?"

"She's staying an extra month - 'til mid-September."

"Oh, I'm delighted pet, why doesn't she move in with you while she's here?"

"She already has!"

"Good. I hate you being all alone in that house." Joanna picked up a stick and threw it into the water. Simba loped after it. She remembered, as a child, always wondering if Simba had thoughts - real thoughts. She still couldn't decide. She looked at her small, wiry Mum. Hair colour still the same startling auburn as her own. No additives. Her face weathered and tanned. Joanna's was paler - smoother - and her hair much longer. She wondered what her mother was thinking. As much a mystery as Simba.

Her mother smiled at her. A smile that had warmed with age. A smile that only recently learned to use its eyes.

For one mad moment she wanted to tell her mother - tell her everything - about Helen - about herself, but Simba was at her feet, shaking water and sand all over her and the moment passed. Thankfully.

"Let's go back Mum."

As she drove to the pub she wondered why she didn't tell her mother. Why she hadn't told anyone. Hadn't told anyone about the happiest thing that had ever happened her. She wondered was she afraid to admit she had fallen in love with a woman, with her best friend. Or was it that she felt it too ... fragile, too new? She didn't know. One part of her wanted to scream it aloud to everyone she met. Another part was afraid of mentioning it at all.

A group of her friends were already there when she arrived. Spirits were high. Hugs and kisses all around.

"Where have you been?"

"Have you been working day and night as usual?"

"A new man I suppose?"

She answered honestly - explaining that Helen was home and they spent as much time as possible together. She drank her first gin fast and kept looking at the door.Helen arrived and saw her immediately. They smiled. More greetings and hugs and some handshakes - from blow-ins over the last year.

They sat apart. Not wanting to but feeling they should.

They looked at each other often, pretended to be interested in the surrounding conversations and drank - probably too much. Eventually Helen moved in to where Joanna was sitting. She put her hand under Joanna's thigh.

"I can't stand this - I want to be alone with you. I can't stand not being able to touch you." She smiled through gritted teeth - pretending they were having a normal conversation.

"I can't stand it either - but don't you dare do anything outrageous." Same false smile.

"*Moi!*" She did her Miss Piggy voice. "I wouldn't dream of it."

The party was lively. Old boyfriends asked them to dance - and they did, always looking over their partner's shoulder to see how the other was doing.

They continued drinking, and got a little drunk, even careless.

But no one noticed. No one saw how Joanna's hand touched the back of Helen's neck - and how Helen's eyes closed involuntarily as it did.

No one, that is, except Kathy. Kathy who knew them both so well, who'd grown up with them, gone to school with them, been on holidays with them.

Yes Kathy noticed, but wasn't quite sure what it was, exactly, that she saw.

When Joanna was dancing with Geoff, who had a new girlfriend at last, Helen signalled with her eyes for her to follow. She did.

"What's wrong?" Joanna asked outside the bathroom door. Helen pulled her into the bathroom, locked the door, threw her arms around her friend and kissed her.

"Absolutely nothing - nothing at all," she said through her kisses.

A few minutes later there was a knock on the door.

"Hurry up whoever's there - I'm dying to go."

"It's Gyrating Geoff" giggled Helen.

"Coming" Joanna called, disentangling herself from Helen.

"Well we would be if you'd leave us alone Geoffrey darling," Helen giggled.

"SShhh" said Joanna.

"Who's in there?" shouted Geoff.

"Me" said Joanna.

"Us" said Helen.

"Hurry up in there," said a strange voice.

Joanna turned the key. Well Joanna didn't turn the key, because the key was stuck. A third male voice had joined the others outside. "What's all the commotion?"

"The lock is jammed," Joanna called.

Groans all round.

"Who's in there?"

"Push the key under the door."

"It's Helen and Joanna."

"Together!"

"No push it under the door - we'll try it from the outside."

"What's going on guys - an orgy?" Kathy's voice.

Joanna pushed the key under the door. Helen, perched on the side of the bath grabbed her around the waist and pulled her - Geoff took the key and put it in the keyhole. Joanna stumbled backwards knocking Helen into the empty bath. Geoff pushed the door open

- hard - the door caught Joanna's legs - Joanna's legs kicked over the shelf above the bath. Geoff, Kathy, Declan (the unidentified voice) and a stranger pushed into the tiny bathroom together just in time to see Joanna, on top of Helen, in the empty bath - legs everywhere and covered in shampoo and conditioner and toothpaste and whatever else happened to be on the shelf.

Everyone began laughing - almost hysterically - except Kathy, who smiled, slowly.

* * *

The following Friday Joanna said goodbye to Helen before leaving for work.

"You'll be back on Tuesday?"

"Yes - can I come here if it's not too late?"

Joanna looked at her incredulously.

"Whaddyamean, 'Can I come here?' You live here. In fact - don't eat and I'll cook. We can have a bottle of wine."

"Great - I'll try to make sure I'm here before nine."

Joanna worked late that night and went out for a few drinks with Derek - who quizzed her about her new lover. She was evasive and they laughed about it.

For the first time since she'd moved into her house she thought it a bit lonely. She switched on all the lamps and made coffee. She wondered what Helen was doing now. Probably asleep. She put on Jennifer Warnes and gazed out the window at the half moon. She thought, "That's how I feel moon-halved."

In her cold unwelcoming bed she picked up pen and paper and wrote to her friend and lover - honestly. Telling her what she did that day and how lonely she was now. She wrote too about the fear. The fear that was beginning to cover her like a blanket. The fear of Helen leaving.

The phone rang. One thirty am. It was Helen.

She slept easy but woke early and reached out - to nothing. The weekend dragged by. She decided to work both days. Getting up early, not wanting to rest on in bed alone, immediately putting on the radio or a cassette - wishing away the quietness. She was trying to write a half-hour documentary script but found the orange letters on her word processor jumbling in front of her eyes. Her mind kept drifting. She'd look at the clock often and wonder what Helen would be doing right now. She laboured through the script sentence by sentence and was unhappy with the end result. She couldn't muster up the enthusiasm to go out at night and just sat in front of the fire watching TV.

On Sunday night, quite late, the phone rang. Again she ran to pick it up.

"Hello - Helen?" Static. "Hello - is that you Helen?" she said again.

"Hello." A French accent, it was him, Laurent.

"Hello - Joanna is that you?"

"Yes Laurent - how are you?" she half shouted down the phone.

"I'm fine - and you?"

"Helen isn't here Laurent - she's away with her parents for the weekend."

"Oh, that's why there's no reply there."

"She'll be back on Tuesday evening - will I get her to call you?"

"Not specially Joanna. Tell her I got her letter, I believe she's staying for another month."

"Yes," she replied a little warily.

"I trust you to keep an eye on her Joanna - don't let her go running off with any of her old boyfriends," he laughed.

He was a very self-assured man.

Joanna laughed too.

"Don't worry - I'll make damn sure she doesn't."

That night Helen didn't call and Joanna cried herself to sleep.

* * *

Tuesday arrived eventually. Joanna stopped in the supermarket on the way home. She bought food, a good bottle of red and one of white wine. She bought fresh candles. Cleaned the sitting-room, lit the fire, and with Ella Fitzgerald for company she prepared fruit and salads, garlic potatoes and cream chicken. Chilled the white. Opened the red. And got into the shower.

In her bedroom she stopped at the mirror. She had been walking around the room naked. Something she never did - not without criticising herself. She smiled at her reflection. For the first time she saw small, firm, attractive. Not the usual bony shapelessness. She dressed in black. Black fine cotton shirt, with a brooch at the neck, black tailored trousers, black suede shoes and a black silk scarf tying her hair back loosely. She liked the look. She was amused at the amount of fuss she was making. Fuss she'd never made for a man in her life! She lit the candles. Poured a glass of wine and sat, trying to concentrate on Anita Brookner's latest.

At eight forty five she heard the car.

"I'm not going to run to the door" she thought - thinking herself ridiculous.

Key in door - door opening - closing. "Joanna?"

"In here." She stood.

Helen walked in. Weekend bag in hand. She looked stunning. All in white - setting off her darkness. They looked at each other - didn't touch - didn't speak. Each appraising the other.

"You look beautiful."

"So do you," Joanna replied, wishing she'd got there first.

When they did hug, Helen caught their reflection in the full-length mirror.

"Look." She said.

They did look stunning - both of them. Such contrasts. White and black. Dark and pale. Silky smooth and wild.

Over dinner Joanna told of Laurent's phone call. All Helen said was "OK." And went on to talk about the weekend and her parents.

"Helen?" Joanna asked after a few glasses of wine. "What are we going to do? What's going to happen?"

Helen didn't speak.

"I mean, you're going back to Hong Kong - to Laurent. What's going to happen to us?"

"Yes, I'm going back to Hong Kong and ..." she stopped and looked at Joanna pleadingly "and, oh God Joanna, I don't know what's going to happen. Maybe this will go on forever. Or maybe, by necessity, it will stop. I don't know. I just don't know. I don't want it to stop. But who knows? I'm leaving. God knows what you're going to do. Who you're going to start seeing when I'm away." She was near tears. "I love him - you do know that I love him, don't you? But loving him, I don't know how I can fall in love with someone else. And having fallen in love with you I don't know how I can love you both at the same time. But I do. He seems very far away right now. But I know that I love him ..." She trailed off.

Joanna looked down at her hands and realised that this was the first time - consciously - she wished Helen had said something different.

"Would you be jealous of me with someone else Helen?"

"I know it's totally unreasonable, but I was thinking about it this weekend, and yes I would a bit. Not so much if it was a man. But I think I'd go mad at the thought of you with another woman."

Joanna laughed. "That's highly unlikely."

And they began to talk about ex-boyfriends, and their first-ever kisses.

They danced to the Eurythmics. Threw cushions in front of the fire. Took off their clothes. Drank wine from each other's mouths. And watched themselves making love in the mirror, surrounded by flickering light from candles and fire.

Helen knelt - arms stretched out. Hands flat on the broad, full length mirror. Legs slightly parted - hair falling into her eyes. Joanna moulded into her back - holding her hips. Moving them slowly - rhythmically. She stared at herself. Nipples hard. Body stretching back into Joanna's. Their eyes met.

"Just watch yourself." Joanna's voice spoke quietly over Annie Lennox.

Joanna moved her hands slowly, gently, along Helen's hips, onto her stomach, back to her sides - barely skimming the edges of her breasts. Then around her back to her shoulders and down her arms. Her softness encompassing Helen's back as their hands met briefly at the mirror. She drew one hand along the underside of an arm and touched Helen's breast -

lightly. The other hand she brought to Helen's face, where each finger was taken luxuriously into her mouth, one by one. Her wet fingers moved to her breast.

Helen took her hands away from the mirror and pulled Joanna towards her.

"Put your hands back - look."

Helen smiled. "I think you got there Joanna."

Later Helen saw her own expression, of near pain, as her body stiffened then relaxed - induced by Joanna's gentle then urgent caresses. The certain touch that instinctively 'knew'.

"Maybe we've been in love for years and just never realised," one of them said.

# Chapter Seven

They were happy that Summer.

They became used to each other - almost. Sometimes they would study each other - when the other wasn't aware - and wonder at what they were doing - wonder at how they came to be together. Occasionally sex made them shy - almost embarrassed, like teenagers just discovering their sexuality. But *never* did it feel wrong. Never.

They would choose a novel together and Helen would read aloud from it. Joanna would sit behind her, hear the words, listen to the story. She loved it - she'd never been read to as a child. And then they'd discuss it - see who could guess what happened next.

And she read to Helen - badly - in French - from *Bonjour Tristesse*. And this she'd haltingly try to translate - embarrassing herself with her mistakes. Helen never laughed at her - she'd put her hand on her arm and smile encouragingly. "Go on - you're going great," and try to explain the complex tenses - and how easy they were really!

"Helen, my problem is I don't even understand English grammar." They laughed and went back to the beginning - Helen teaching her both English and French grammar together.

Sometimes Joanna felt she had nothing to give - nothing real. So she lavished love and more love on her. *And* treated them both to lovely evenings out at concerts and dinners - anything and everything.

Joanna hadn't painted in years - not since school.

One day - looking at Helen - lying naked on top of the duvet, reading to her, she decided to take out her paints.

And she painted, long full strokes of the brush in pinks, yellows, mauves. She put her lover's curves on canvas - in bright bright colours, not even giving in to darkness for Helen's black hair. And she listened, not hearing the story, just the words, as Helen continued reading.

Helen thought the painting beautiful - and it was. Joanna inscribed the back of it.

"For Helen with love and and and".

In restaurants at night, sitting talking over dinner and wine, they never noticed the inquisitive waiters and waitresses who watched them carefully and discussed with their colleagues if 'they were or weren't'. Never noticed young men at other tables shaking hands, congratulating each other when either of them made a gesture that meant 'they were'. And inevitably they always did make a gesture that meant 'they were'. Generally a move or a caress made by Helen - accepted shyly by Joanna.

They didn't notice the shocked looks on the young women's faces standing behind them at the Queen concert. Shocked at the way Helen stood behind Joanna, arms wrapped so comfortably around her - moving to the rhythm of the music. Occasionally stroking back her auburn hair to shout something in her ear, and then kissing her cheek. Like any new lovers really.

They didn't notice much. And all too soon, frighteningly too soon it was September. Mid-September. They never spoke of it. Both of them aware but frightened of what faced them. Frightened of leaving one another but feeling they had no option. This was not the way it was supposed to be!

Helen already had a lover, a man she loved. This love of theirs would have to remain a secret. And Joanna was too unsure of her place in Helen's life to talk about it. Helen was going back to Laurent and her job in Hong Kong so that must be what she wanted to do. Joanna found herself wanting to say "Helen don't go," or "Let me come with you." But she didn't say it. She was scared of what was happening to them but even more scared of losing what they'd just found.

She knew she wanted children.

She knew that 'homosexual' or 'lesbian' were dirty words in Ireland. So she put it all to the back of her mind. But not what she felt for Helen.

Helen said she'd be home at Christmas. Joanna said

nothing. Thought nothing. She needed to deaden her mind too, to thoughts of loneliness, of jealousy. Thoughts that lurked threateningly somewhere in her head. "Plenty of time for those thoughts when she's gone." Somehow they didn't argue or get sad. They remained best friends, lovers - even with the impending departure, the confusion and the secrecy. They had close friends in for drinks two nights before she left. Their last night was for Helen's family and for them, alone.

* * *

"Why don't we go out on Sunday night Joanna, after Helen leaves?" Kathy asked her. "We could go for a meal and catch up - I feel as if we haven't really talked in months."

Joanna smiled at her gratefully and accepted. Kathy touched her arm and kissed her forehead - an unusual action for her, for them.

The night before Helen left, Joanna sat on her bed and watched her pack her suitcase. Neither of them felt the usual excitement of a trip. They were very quiet.

Joanna handed her the letter she'd been writing since their weekend apart.

"You can read it on the plane - not before. It's just things, feelings, things I couldn't really bring myself to say."

Helen smiled, took the letter and handed Joanna an envelope. "I did exactly the same - read it when I'm gone."

That night they lay awake talking for hours like when they were teenagers. When the light began to rise they noticed it was four am and began singing the

Leonard Cohen song.

*"It's four in the morning, the end of December, I'm writing you now just to see if you're better."*

They sang the whole song, very quietly, arms around each other, while the sky outside got brighter and nature began to wake, just as they were about to sleep.

Helen's parents brought her to the airport. Joanna and Helen preferred it that way. When she knew Helen had boarded she sat in the garden and read her letter.

*15 September*

*My dear sweet Joanna,*
*When you read this I will be on my way back to my other lover. I can only try to imagine how you must feel. But what other way is there? None. We know that. Oh God - I don't know how I feel about anything any more. I know that I love you more than I could ever have imagined. That I know.*
*Where did all this love come from? Why must it hurt so much? The thought of leaving you is already tearing me apart.*
*And you my love - how must you feel now, reading this?*
*Oh Joanna, be OK. Please be OK. I will write often - and I'll see you in three months. We thought five days was long. How am I going to manage three months? I won't have you to talk to - to tell my every thought. And I won't be able to talk about you either - not in any real way.*
*How will we be when we see each other again? What is going to happen? Don't hate me for leaving, Darling. You know I have to - I'm sorry. I'm so damned*

*confused.*
*Goodbye for now my new found lover and forever friend*

*HELEN*
*XXXXXX*

She didn't feel the rain in the cool breeze, or notice that the sun had hidden behind a huge black cloud as she sat on the base of a tree stump, sobbing.

* * *

Kathy called in at seven that night.

"Jesus, Joanna you look terrible" she said as her friend, paler than usual, opened the door.

"Thanks a lot," she smiled falsely. "You look great."

Kathy tiptoed around her conversationally - asking, casually only, about Helen. Eventually, at the end of the meal Kathy put her hand on Joanna's saying softly,

"Do you want to tell me Joanna?"

Joanna, who had been near to tears all evening, let them spill out.

Kathy paid the bill and led her out of the restaurant. The other customers pretended not to notice the young woman so obviously distraught. They were embarrassed for her and wondered what made her so upset - each imagining a different story.

People who didn't know Kathy often misunderstood her - thought her bossy. She wasn't bossy. She was straightforward and honest. A big woman - tall and large-boned with regular features and mid brown hair - and a smile that could knock you flat, it was so broad. And penetrating grey eyes. Kathy loved Joanna. Always had, as long as she could remember. She thought her vulnerable and sort of 'special'. She never could successfully describe what she meant by 'special'. She just knew it .

She took charge. Put Joanna sitting in front of the fire and made two Irish coffees. Sat opposite her and said "OK Joanna, from the beginning."

Joanna talked and told and cried - for two solid hours. With the barest of probing from Kathy. When she'd finished she looked at Kathy - expecting the worst. She felt totally drained - worn out - could barely lift her third Irish coffee to her lips. At this stage she didn't really care what anyone thought.

"My poor Joanna - it must be rough," was all she said.

Joanna looked at her sharply. "You don't need to pretend not to be disgusted you know."

"Don't ever say anything like that to me again," Kathy snapped at her. "Don't *ever* put me into a box that says this woman is so damned straight she couldn't see love if it bit her on the nose. It's not fair and you know it. *I have known* about the two of you for ages".

Joanna was visibly shocked.

"It's so obvious - to me anyway. It's not disgusting. OK - so maybe it's not for me - not my way. But it doesn't mean I can't understand it." She sighed and her voice softened. "Look Joanna, all I think is that it's sad - sad and wrong."

Joanna looked at her questioningly.

"I don't understand how she could fall in love with you and then leave you."

"Well what else could she have done?" Joanna asked, annoyed.

"Left him and stayed with you of course, or asked you to go with her or whatever."

"But how could we live together, as lovers, I mean? There's never been any question of either her leaving him or of us living together. Never."

"Well why the hell hasn't there been? What do you think you've been doing for the past few months? Playing a game?"

Joanna shrugged.

"And why not live together? You two are always claiming to be so damned liberal. Why the hell not? Lesser beings have done it you know."

She went to bed drained. Kathy stayed in the spare room. Eventually she fell asleep with Helen's letter still in her hand. And the question 'Why not?' racing around her head.

When she woke the first thing she noticed was a sort of awareness. An awareness of loss? She didn't reach out for Helen. Even in her sleep she was sure she was alone. Her head felt dull and her body heavy.

She rang the office from the phone beside her bed and told Derek that she wouldn't be in for a few days - everything would simply have to wait. Derek sounded anxious. She thought it was because she was missing work and snapped at him. "I'm sick Derek - can't I be bloody sick for once!"

She got up and made breakfast for Kathy, who was going to be late for work.

"Kathy, I'm going away for a few days. Alone. I need to think."

Kathy was worried, but late. "Promise you won't do anything stupid OK?"

"I promise. I'll only be a couple of days."

A few hours later she was in her car, driving north to Donegal. She drove in silence. No music, no radio. Luckily, the house was free. Mrs O'Reilly thought it was very strange that she should want to stay there alone, and told her so.

She threw her bag on the floor of their bedroom - lay face down on the bed and cried. Loudly. Quietly. Hysterically. Silently.

She didn't bother to wash her tearstained face when she went to sit on her rock. It was dusk. The sun was setting behind her as she looked out to sea. A cold breeze burnt her hot cheeks. She felt none of the breathless exhilaration she was used to feeling, looking at such beauty. The only chill along her spine was from the cold.

And peace of mind! There was none. She knew the sun was a fiery red now. She could see it casting colours on the hills miles and miles away with startling clarity. The sea was calm. Only 'whooshing' against the rocks. And she smiled - an inward smile. The 'whooshing' reminded her of her school playground. She wondered did Helen ever think of that.

It was nearly dark when she walked back to the house, along the hard sand of the lagoon. "Full out now - full in at three am and three pm. Maybe I'll swim tomorrow."

Getting into bed she noticed that the moon was only a sliver and thought she was like the moon but hoped not because the moon had always been alone. She woke often. Nervous of being in the house on her own. Frightened of the shadows on the wall and the windows rattling in the light wind.

She got up late, with the same feeling as the previous

morning. Moved around the big house feeling insecure - lonely. Maybe that's what the dull thudding in her head and the ache in her chest was - loneliness. She rattled around the house for four days. Sitting out on her rock, reading occasionally, writing often, manically - to herself - to Helen. Tearing up most of the pages to Helen because on re-reading them she realised her words were desperate, out of control, sometimes angry. But mostly desperate.

*You've really made a mess of all this now haven't you? Falling for your best friend! Will you ever learn? Your best female friend, and she already with a male lover. You're obsessed with her. Completely obsessed. And where is she? Away - miles away - in Hong Kong - with her man. And where are you? Stuck here going mad. Neglecting your work. Neglecting your friends. Neglecting your house. Get it together woman!*

But she couldn't.

Pulling up outside her front door in Dublin, she noticed for the second time that Summer, that she didn't care about it any more. The house that she'd struggled so hard to buy. So important to her, symbol of her total independence.

The phone was ringing when she opened the door. In her haste she didn't notice the post on the floor.

"Joanna, where the hell have you been?" It was Kathy. Angry.

"I told you I was going away for a couple of days," she said defensively.

"Sure you did. But a couple means *two* - you were gone for *four*. And you only told me, you idiot. Your mother is frantic."

"Oh God, did she call you?"

"Yes she called me - and so did Derek." Her voice was calming, "and so did Helen."

"Helen called?"

"Yes, and she's worried sick about you - you should call her."

Silence.

"Joanna, I told her that I knew the whole story."

"Oh God, what did she say?"

"She said she was glad and that I was to take care of you until she came home."

Silence.

"She misses you Joanna."

"I know, I can feel it."

Kathy became businesslike again "Will you get your act together - call everybody and come over for a drink."

"I don't really feel like going ..."

"I don't care what you feel like - get your ass in gear and get over here." Click.

She went out to close the front door and picked up her post. Access - damn. Telephone - damn. Postcard, Helen - hooray. Visa - oh well. Letter, Helen - fantastic.

The thudding that had been in her head since Sunday began to ease. Miraculously.

The card didn't say much except that she'd arrived safely and missed her and loved her. The letter spoke of desolation and real longing. It spoke so explicitly of the night they made love in front of the mirror that Joanna felt her cheeks grow hot.

She got her diary to check Helen's number and dialled.

After four rings it was picked up.

"Hello?"

She froze. For a split second she'd forgotten his

existence.

"Hello, hello, who's there?"

"Hello Laurent, it's me, Joanna."

"Oh, Joanna," he sounded warm. "How are you?"

"Fine, just fine thanks - and you?"

"Very well, now that I have Helen back. You had her just a little bit too long for my liking this time." He laughed. "But I'm glad you called, she's been missing you," ever confident. "You ran off for a few days?"

"Yes."

"With a lucky man?"

"No Laurent, with myself."

"Oh ... you must come over to us soon Joanna. I'd love to get to know you better. I'm always hearing so much about you and we've only met the one time. It seems ridiculous don't you think?" His English, perfect as usual.

"Yes, maybe if I get time off work."

They hadn't moved in together had they? They couldn't have. Not so soon!

"Ah yes, always working too hard - you liberated women."

"So, you've finally moved in together," she ventured, laughing nervously.

"No, no, I'm afraid not. She's a very cautious woman. Maybe you could put in a good word for me?" He laughed. "Hold on and I'll get her for you."

She could hear him calling out to her in French, then leaving the room and closing the door, considerately, as Helen picked up the receiver.

They talked - like lovers - of how they missed one another. They even laughed at Laurent's innocence. When they hung up Joanna felt warmed. Desolation and headache both gone, she made her calls, soothingly, convincingly. Even Kathy was taken in by her good form.

It didn't last long. Her life became ruled by the P&T. She would wake feeling stricken. If there was no post from Helen it would worsen as the day went on. If there was a letter, the day would become bearable. She found that she couldn't concentrate and her work suffered. Her mind couldn't stay on one thing for any period of time. She was always drifting into thoughts of Helen. Remembering over and over again things they had done in the summer. Imagining what they would do when they saw each other next. Sometimes even trying to imagine them living together - for real. She didn't often think of that. She felt it would probably never happen and pushed it away, along with thoughts of Laurent.

Luckily she got letters - often - long letters full of wanting and missing. She wrote back as many, sometimes more. The more they wrote to one another, the more apparent it became to both of them that a choice, a decision, would have to be made. That the 'triangle' could not work. They were amazed at their previous innocence. How could they have imagined it could have worked, they said often. Helen becoming aware, slowly, along with her confusion. And Joanna in full awareness of what was happening, because of her desolation.

She tried to explain to Kathy how she felt.

"It's just that I was so happy with her. Happy like I've never felt before. I felt as if I ... belonged. I still feel I belong - not that she owns me - but that by will I belong *with* her, not to her. And when she's not here I feel disconnected. As if I've lost my roots. Nowhere is home anymore. And it's not because she's physically not here. If she was simply away, and I knew she was coming back - to me - I wouldn't care. Sure, I'd miss her. But I wouldn't care. But the fear of losing her is eating me up. Eating me up and turning my brains to shit."

"You won't lose her Joanna. I know you won't. I've seen you both together. I don't know *any* man who could compete with that."

"Unfortunately he doesn't seem to be just *any* man."

* * *

The days dragged by. She earmarked everything from 'the day Helen left' and counted the days to her return. She wanted to see her. To see if it was still real. And during one lonesome conversation it was decided. Helen had a chance of going to a conference in San Francisco for a week in November. She asked Joanna to come over.

"To San Francisco?" Joanna asked incredulously.

"I really need to see you." Helen replied. "Do you think you could take the time off? Could you afford it?"

"Well, yes and yes I suppose." Joanna began to think about it properly. "Yes - I'll come. Definitely. I'm cracking up here without you." She began to get excited at the thought of seeing Helen sooner than she'd expected. "How did this come up? Did the college just land it on you?" she asked.

"I've known about it for ages but I wasn't going to go - they're only partially funding it you see."

"Oh, can *you* afford it? I mean if you need any money I can send some over."

"No, no, I'll be fine. Don't worry. Sure if I need to I can borrow it from Laurent!" she said mischeviously.

"You're still a bad bitch Helen, you know that."

Joanna hung up and in her usual whirlwind fashion had organised a flight, a car, and six days off work within a few hours. Then she called to tell Helen of her arrival in three weeks - 21 days. She felt lightheaded. Helen missed her just as much - wanted to see her.

Derek was worried and he told her.

"You seem ... different these days Joanna. Are you alright?"

"I'm fine," she replied, smiling reassuringly.

"The time off isn't a problem - you know how to manage that best yourself. I know I've said it before but you do seem distracted."

"I know Derek" she conceded. "Everything is a bit difficult these days. But I swear I'll be back on form when I get back. I need to sort things out, you know?"

"Well no, I don't know Joanna. You don't have to tell me if you don't want to. But what's going on?"

Joanna sat down - she'd been standing in the doorway of his office.

"You know this 'lover' of mine?" Derek nodded. "Well this person does not live here." He nodded again. "In fact this person lives thousands of miles away and already has a ... partner."

"Oh! I'm sorry Joanna."

"So am I Derek. But we're trying to sort things out."

She got up to leave.

"You don't deserve that Joanna. You deserve someone who loves you and only you."

She smiled at him and felt a bit sad.

Derek worried even more before she left. She worked like a maniac. It was as if this lover of hers was controlling the amount of air she had to breathe. She worked until midnight most nights, and most weekends too. All the programmes she was putting together were fastmoving - almost unbearably so. Each scene was gone, almost before it had time to register. But it worked - the programmes were fantastic. Each half hour felt like ten minutes. One night she was so tired that she left an entire page of script out of the programme. But the rest was so good that Derek didn't care about the six hours extra editing the mistake had created.

Kathy worried about her. Her mother hardly saw her. And whenever anyone did see her she was in extreme high humour, and they thought she was in 'fantastic form'. She thought so too.

The days passed on a high and soon she was off. Kathy dropped her to the airport and hugged her hard when she was leaving. Joanna half ran through the barrier, waving and beaming at Kathy, not even noticing that she was flirting with the security man.

# Chapter Eight

Normally she loved travelling. Not this time. She couldn't help but feel that every moment spent in an airport or on a plane was time without Helen. She had to fly to London first, stay the night in a hotel and then take off for San Francisco early next morning. It was a twelve hour flight - her longest so far. She'd been to New York a few times before, but never to the West Coast.

The hotel in London was awful. Big, impersonal and crowded. She didn't want to meet up with any of her friends so she stayed in her characterless room and waxed her legs, shaved her underarms and made a big fuss about getting her hair to look as 'naturally wild' as possible. All that done, she studied herself in the mirror and decided what she would wear the next day, choosing Helen's favourite clothes. They were her favourite too. A very old pair of faded jeans and a black cotton crew neck.

That night she slept badly. The bed was hard - the room too warm - the walls too thin.

In the early hours of the morning she woke to the sound of fighting in the next room. Male voices. Very drunk.

Eventually she drifted into a light sleep.

In the morning she stood in the lobby with other travellers, waiting for the hotel bus to bring them to Terminal Four. She studied them, wondering if any of them would be travelling with her to San Francisco. She wore a watch travelling - the only time she ever did. And she looked at it often, counting the hours to her arrival, subtracting eight hours so she'd know what Helen was doing. 'Fast asleep now' she thought to herself .

She got a middle seat on the plane and cursed herself for forgetting to ask for the window. There was a grey haired attractive older woman on her left who had taken off her shoes and smiled at Joanna brightly as she squashed past the middle-aged, unmistakably American man who was seated on her right. She put on her headphones as soon as she was settled but knew it would be difficult to avoid conversation on such a long flight.

She was right. As they were taking off, the woman beside her grasped Joanna's forearm and said, "This is my first time in a plane."

Joanna patted her arm reassuringly and talked to her until they were in the air.

'Elizabeth' and herself became great friends for the next twelve hours. Elizabeth told Joanna about the son she was going to visit in California. She hadn't seen him in fifteen years and had never met her grandchildren. Joanna didn't ask the obvious 'why?' - really not wanting to know. And Elizabeth asked Joanna who the lucky person receiving such a long letter was. Joanna lied about it - not wanting to explain that she was writing to the person who was meeting her at the airport.

The flight seemed endless and Joanna drifted in and out of semi-sleep, mainly when Elizabeth was talking too much.

When they finally landed, Joanna had a desperate urge to jump over the backs of the seats past the huge queue of people, but knew there was no point as she'd still have to go through immigration and then wait for her baggage.

Immigration was much faster than New York had ever been. But it seemed like an age before she saw her bag crawl its way up through the hole in the airport floor and wend its way towards her. She grabbed it and raced through 'Nothing to Declare' toward the exit door. It slid open. A mass of waiting faces. It slowed her down. Where was Helen? She couldn't see her. She was walking slower now. The noise was deafening. Flight announcements, excited greetings.

Helen had seen her and was running to her. Suddenly she was there. They stood for a moment, just looking at one another, not touching, prolonging the moment. Then Joanna dropped her bags as Helen reached out and they engulfed each other in a hug that was warm, exciting and secure. Neither of them spoke. They couldn't. They were both smiling and crying, unable to form sentences. Eventually they made their way to the Avis desk to pick up their rented Chevy.

Joanna drove. She needed something to concentrate on to steady her hands and her breathing. Helen had booked them into a guest house in the city. And had worked out the route from the airport to the house. But sometimes she was staring so hard at Joanna that she missed a couple of turns, making their journey longer than necessary. But neither of them cared. They were together now. They sat as far away from each other as two people sitting in the front seats of the same car possibly can. Not touching. Almost afraid of what would happen if they did.

The 'Inn San Francisco' was a big old house with too many steps up to the front door. The owners were proud of its age - old houses are hard to come by in San Francisco - and they took Joanna, Helen and a middle-aged couple on a guided history tour of the house.

But Joanna and Helen weren't listening to the articulate young woman's description of the wood in the walls in the dining-room. The woman, Louise, proudly presented their newly installed jacuzzi. It was the only time Helen spoke.

"Is this open through the night?" she asked Louise while gazing directly at Joanna.

It wasn't.

"What a pity." She grinned boldly.

Joanna stared at the ground trying to stifle her laugh - barely succeeding.

Eventually they were shown to their room. It had a massive four poster bed in it, two windows and a basin. They stood at opposite sides of the bed and smiled shyly at each other, still unsure of how to be, what to do, unable to express out loud how they felt, afraid that the other didn't feel the same.

Joanna broke the silence.

"Will we go out? It's a beautiful day and you've to show me the sights."

Helen loved the city. She'd spent a summer there in her third year of college. They took a bus - parking was too hard to find. Joanna normally hated waiting for buses but today she didn't care. There was so much to see. San Francisco was so multi-racial, but not in the same way as London somehow.

It was sunny and cool. The sky was the startlingly clear blue of a sunny winter day at home. No clouds. And the city was quietly noisy - unlike New York. Here, there was a constant background hum of activity, interrupted only occasionally by the odd siren or car horn. Helen leaned against Joanna as they waited for the bus. They didn't talk. It was the same on the bus. Helen speaking only to give a brief account of the journey and trying desperately to remember which stop to get off at.

An old white haired, white-faced woman shouted obscenities at the young Native American boy who offered her his seat.

"Little bastard. You and your kind think you can take over our country."

Joanna was shocked. She wanted to hit the old bag. Helen hadn't heard and couldn't figure out why Joanna was so agitated.

"What's wrong?" she asked when they got off the bus. Joanna told her - Helen smiled. "It's awful isn't it, but what's even more awful is that you get so used to it you barely even notice."

Joanna thought she would *never* get used to it.

They walked the streets - Helen testing out her memory. Only going into places that interested them - no touristy sightseeing. An art gallery that hung dozens of paintings, all of the same woman. An electrical shop that sold executive toys and gadgets.

"I'll have to look for something for Derek." Joanna went inside.

"Feel this." Helen said as she rubbed a body massager across the back of Joanna's neck.

"It feels wonderful, how much is it?"

"Eighty dollars."

"Oh ... it doesn't feel *that* wonderful."

A little while later Helen found Joanna staring, almost trancelike, at a see-through globe that had forks of lightning striking out from the gas centre. If you touched the glass the forks would latch onto your fingertips and move with them and then calm when you removed your hand. She sensed Helen behind her and reached back.

"Look Helen, it's like us, cocooned in our own world that people can only see and never really get into," she whispered.

Helen squeezed her hand tightly, and if Joanna hadn't had her back turned she would have seen the frightened expression on Helen's face, who was thinking that Joanna was right, they were like the 'illumina storm' and everyone, even Laurent, could only touch the outside. Surely that couldn't be right? She pushed the thought away.

"How much is it?"

"Three hundred dollars" Joanna said turning around. "A bit too extravagant, even for Derek don't you think?"

They stopped in a deli for a snack. One that had

trays and trays of colourful fresh fruit outside and a huge variety of salads and cold meats inside. Joanna hadn't eaten properly since she'd left Ireland, but her stomach was upset so she toyed with her salad.

"Let's go back to the 'Inn' soon, book a table in some restaurant, have a shower and go out." Helen suggested.

"OK. I'm sure I'll be starving by then."

She was feeling tired now from her travelling. A shower would wake her up.

When they got back they went up to the roof garden to look over the city. Joanna stood with her elbows on the wall and squinted at the long evening shadows. She closed her eyes to savour the sounds and smells of the day. The distant hum and the very faint smell of food rising from the streets. Helen came and stood behind her, wrapping her arms around her shoulders.

Joanna thought "I'm so happy."

"What did you say?" Helen asked.

Joanna hadn't spoken out loud, but she wasn't surprised that Helen thought she had.

"I'm happier than I've ever been in my life."

Helen turned her around and kissed her and they could feel their bodies exhale in relief with that kiss.

The door to their room closed, they slowly undressed each other, not speaking at all.

It was dark outside when Joanna spoke.

"We have a few things to sort out, don't we Helen?" she said gently as she stroked Helen's inner arm. "Yes we do ... well *I* do. It's me really isn't it?"

Joanna nodded. They sat up in the bed.

"I needed to see you Joanna, so badly. I missed you. I didn't know I could miss a person so much." She smiled. "But I needed to see you too, to see, to know if it was real. You know?" She looked at Joanna for understanding. Joanna nodded and pulled her close.

"Well?" Joanna said "Is it real?" Knowing the answer.

"You know it is."

She framed Joanna's face in her hands. "But this being real doesn't make anything else disappear. It doesn't make Laurent disappear."

"I know that Helen. I know that."

Helen kissed her.

"What I'm asking you for is time. I can't make a decision about all this right now. I need to sort it out, make sense of it - in my own head."

Joanna returned her kiss.

"Time is something I've got a lot of. Take all the time you need."

In the morning they got up, showered and went downstairs for breakfast. Joanna was starving and piled her plate high with pineapple, hard boiled egg and croissant. She thought it a peculiar combination for breakfast but it tasted good. She poured two mugs of steaming coffee and sat on a couch beside Helen who was already studying a map of California. They were to plan the remaining five days together.

"I want to see Lake Tahoe - I never got a chance the last time I was here." Helen said.

"I just want to go wine tasting." Joanna said.

"Bloody typical," Helen laughed, "alcohol on the brain! Both those locations are north of here."

"Why? Where do you go wine tasting?" Joanna asked.

"Napa valley is supposed to be the best."

As they drove to Napa, Joanna said "Oh God Helen,

we've only got five days."

Helen laughed. "You could say we've got all of five days and then it's only five weeks until Christmas."

"Yes, but five weeks is all of thirty five days isn't it?" She smiled a little.

They toured Napa valley taking in five different vineyards and Joanna laughed loudly when she saw the tiny drop of wine that was poured into the bottom of each glass to taste.

"And I thought we'd be rolling home tonight," she said. It was a long day and they were tired at the end of it. They bought three bottles of their favourite wines and sat quietly with their purchases outside a café drinking coffee. The wine had, after all, gone to their heads.

"This place is beautiful isn't it?" Helen said about the open air arcade surrounding them.

"Yes it's fabulous. I love noisy, colourful places."

"Laurent would love it here."

Joanna was jarred by the mention of his name. "Oh would he?" she asked casually.

"Yes. We often go shopping in a place like this in Hong Kong." Helen was looking around - not at Joanna. Joanna said nothing.

"Do you want to get something to eat or what?" Helen asked.

"I don't care."

Hearing Joanna's tone she turned to look at her. "Is there something wrong?"

"No, I just don't care if we eat or not."

Helen made the decision and half an hour later they were sitting opposite one another in a fairly expensive, dimly-lit restaurant, ordering from the menu.

Joanna picked at her food.

"Is your meat not good?" Helen asked.

"It's fine."

"Are you not hungry?"

"Not really."

"Are you sick? You haven't eaten all day."

"I'm *fine* Helen," she said sharply.

"What's wrong Joanna? You've been in dreadful form all evening."

"Nothing, nothing's wrong. I'm just tired. Can we go back to the guest house?"

"Sure, of course we can."

Out on the street as they were getting into the car Helen asked again, "What is it Joanna? Tell me please. You're miles away." She touched Joanna's arm but Joanna moved around to the driver's door. She spoke back to Helen over the car roof.

"If you really want to know Helen - *I don't care* what sort of arcade you and Laurent go shopping in, OK?"

She put the key in the lock.

"I thought it must have been that."

"Well, then why did you ask me?" Joanna glared at her, "and why did you say it?"

"Look Joanna, Laurent is important to me. He's a huge part of my life. We can't pretend he doesn't exist."

Joanna flared "*I can* Helen. I can *so easily* pretend that he doesn't exist."

Helen looked stunned.

"How can you pretend he doesn't exist?" she shouted. "How can you pretend that someone I love doesn't exist?"

"Without any problem at all." Joanna replied coldly as she wrenched open the car door.

They drove in silence. Joanna was finding it hard to drive. Her eyes had filled up with tears. She was crying silently. Her hands began to shake. Helen noticed and looked at her face. She softened immediately. "Oh Joanna, don't cry, please don't cry." She wiped the tears from Joanna's face with her fingers. Joanna cried and shook more.

"I *have* to pretend he doesn't exist. I *have* to. To survive - to survive. I can't think about the two of them together. I can't. It frightens me. I feel so jealous. I'm afraid of losing her. What would I do without Helen? What would I do? I'd die. I'd probably die. She's the only one who knows me."

She was talking frantically as if Helen wasn't there. Helen was trying to calm her down but Joanna kept talking quietly to herself and crying.

"Joanna, pull in love." she said it over and over until it finally got through and Joanna pulled in to the side of the road. She lifted the handbrake and fell across it onto Helen's lap.

Helen stroked her hair until the sobbing eased.

"I'm sorry Joanna. I'm so sorry," she kept whispering.

They switched seats and Helen drove them home.

Helen thought Joanna was probably asleep when she came out of the bathroom. She had looked so pale and drained. She knew Joanna wouldn't want to make love so she switched off the lamp and eased her way into the bed alongside her.

Joanna was awake and she wrapped herself around Helen. Then she thanked her for her gentleness in the way she knew Helen wanted.

The next day they both felt wonderful. They had slept

soundly and the night before was already forgotten - well, it wasn't mentioned anyway. They lolled around their room, reading magazines, having a shower, eating breakfast. At midday they headed for lake Tahoe. Joanna navigated. Helen drove.

It was a long journey so they stopped off on the way, in a place called Grass Valley. They wanted to ring ahead and book a B&B.

In a bar they asked a waitress for advice on a place to stay.

"Oh oh ladies," she drawled, shaking her head. "Billy honey," she shouted to the fat man in a red checked shirt leaning on the bar reading a newspaper, "The Tahoe routes are closed today aren't they?"

"Sure are," he called back moving toward their table. "All snowed up." His accent was heavier than those of the San Francisco people. "You ladies lookin' to get to Tahoe?"

"We were hoping to," Helen replied.

"Roads won't be open for a couple of days at least."

"Oh no!" They groaned at each other.

"Nothing wrong with this town here now is there?" He smiled as he pulled out a chair. "Bring over three beers Elly and I'll give these ladies a notion of what goes on around here."

They liked him. He told them where they could stay, where they could eat, where they could hear music and where they could go sightseeing. They had another beer. And took his advice on all counts.

"It looks like a rich version of The Waltons' house" Joanna said delightedly as pulled up outside the rambling wooden guest house.

The owners were young, a man and a woman. The guy showed them around - leaving out the history.

"Help yourselves to a snack and a glass of wine when you come in this evening," he said as he showed them the kitchen.

Their room was bright and spacious and filled with old furniture. And an open fireplace - set. There were candles on the mantelpiece. They opened the door to the bathroom. Huge sinky white towels, brass fittings on everything - even the handle to flush the loo. Soap, shampoo, bath oil, a razor and shaving foam! All in little individually wrapped packages.

Later, after touring the town, they went to a place Billy had recommended. It was full and lively, mostly with people wearing checked shirts. The music hadn't started yet so they sat at a table and ordered some food. The waitress asked them if they were English.

"No, we're Irish," Joanna replied rolling her eyes at Helen.

"Is it not the same thing?" asked the waitress.

"No, it's not," Helen replied this time seeing Joanna's annoyance. "They're different countries."

"Oh yeh, Ireland is the place where all the fighting's going on isn't it?"

Joanna was wishing the woman away. She started shredding her napkin as Helen tried to explain the difference between northern and southern Ireland to the waitress who wasn't really listening. Finally she went off to get their order.

"I really hate that." Joanna said.

"Yes, so do I. But when you think about it it's not surprising is it?"

"What?" Joanna said sharply, stopping her shredding.

"Well, do you know all the different states in the USA?"

"No." Joanna didn't see the point.

Helen went on. "Look at Ireland, it's tiny in comparison to most USA states never mind the entire USA. So, for people to have heard of Ireland at all is pretty good."

"I suppose so." Joanna said, now shredding the shreds.

The waitress returned with their drinks.

"Ireland, huh?" she said while putting down the drinks, slopping Helen's beer onto the table. "Saints and scholars and leprechauns," she said, pronouncing it 'lepreeshuns'.

"Now you've got it." Helen smiled up at her as Joanna bent her head low. She was laughing silently.

Grass Valley was 'redneck country' according to the city Californians. The people were heavy-accented, rugged looking and very white - in both senses. Untanned and un-black. For the most part they were friendly and interested (even if ignorant) about Joanna's and Helen's roots. Later as they leaned on the dark wood bar they answered the same questions over and over about their accents - their reasons for being there - their nationality. They were glad when the music started - a young man and his guitar.

Helen stroked Joanna's arm often, and sometimes her hair. Joanna put her hand on Helen's caressing hand to restrain it.

Helen looked at her "What's wrong?"

"Nothing, it's just all these people."

"What about them?"

"Nothing really. Well ... you know how I am about showing affection in public."

Helen sat back from her. "No Joanna. I don't. Tell me," she said folding her arms.

"There's no need to move away from me," Joanna said feeling suddenly cold and bare. "I just find it difficut to show affection when there's so many people around."

Helen leaned toward her. "*You* weren't showing affection, *I* was." She turned to face the singer.

Joanna leaned over and took her hand. "Don't be annoyed, please."

"I'm not. I just think it's weird that you're conscious of these strangers thinking us lesbians."

Joanna was shocked. "It's not that at all. I don't care what they think - I just don't feel comfortable sometimes."

Helen shook her head and smiled.

"Joanna - it must be that."

They said no more about it and continued to enjoy the evening. It hadn't felt like an argument.

During the music break the bar area filled up with people. Joanna leaned over to Helen and kissed her. A real kiss.

"I *don't* care what anyone thinks. I love you."

Helen smiled. "Thank you" she said simply.

That night they went home feeling completely at one with each other. It was late so they used their key. The house was sleeping. They sat in front of the dying embers of the fire in the sitting-room for a while. Talking about fires, and what drew people to them other than the obvious warmth.

"Let's get some wine, go to our room and light the fire." Helen said.

"Do you think it's OK to light it?"

"Of course it is - it's set."

They poured large glasses of Californian rosé - so cold the glasses frosted up immediately. They lit the fire and the candles and lay on top of the covers talking. Joanna's head resting on Helen's bare stomach. The fire and their desires creating enough warmth for them to fall asleep without getting under the covers.

When they woke the following morning the candles had burnt away, the coals of the fire were grey and the wine glasses empty. The only thing unchanged were their feelings for each other.

Grass Valley was perfectly named. It was greener than any place they'd seen in Ireland. Even in November it was only spotted with auburn. The valley was breathtakingly beautiful and they didn't talk as they drove slowly along the winding road to the river in the heart of it. It was deserted as they'd hoped. They lay on flat rocks on the riverside in the warm, cool sun. They stayed there for the afternoon talking and taking photos, deciding to leave only when the sun was cool.

As they walked back to the car through the forest, Helen called out "Joanna!" She turned. Helen stared at her for a moment. "I love you."

Joanna suddenly realised as she saw Helen's expression that this was the first time Helen had recognised the depth of their love for each other.

The next day they had to go back to San Francisco. Their last full day and night together, for how long?

"I don't want to be without you." Joanna said to Helen as they went to sleep that night.

Helen hugged her close. "Nor do I my love - nor do I."

San Francisco, being San Francisco, kept their spirits high. They returned to the Inn and Louise was there to check them in.

"I presume you don't want another tour?" She smiled at them.

"No thanks" they replied together quickly.

"Can you recommend somewhere for us to go tonight - for a good meal and some jazz maybe?" Helen looked to Joanna for affirmation.

Joanna nodded and said "It's our last night."

"Oh, that's a shame" Louise said, passing them a list of restaurants. "Some of these are good" she marked them off with a pencil, "but maybe you'd prefer to go to a women's club?" She looked up at them openly. They glanced at each other.

"There's quite a good one a couple of blocks away. It has good food."

"No thanks." Joanna said, reading Helen's expression. "Which one of these do you think is best?"

She told them and made the booking. As they were walking up the now familiar stairs Joanna said to Helen "So it's obvious."

Helen put her arm around her shoulders. "Of course it is."

The restaurant was buzzing.

At first they thought it looked too big to be intimate, forgetting their ability to create their own intimacy.

The food wasn't great. Joanna's dish was far too garlicy, but they chose good wine and didn't really care about the food.

Helen reached across and spooned some of the sauce

on Joanna's plate into her mouth.

"It's not good, is it?" she said, taking another spoonful.

"Why are you taking more - it's awful." Joanna laughed.

"Because my dear, there's no garlic in mine and we'd better *both* be smelling and tasting of garlic tonight, don't you think?"

Joanna smiled and wondered to herself, yet again, how all this happened.

Saxophone and piano were the instruments of the evening. Well played and loud. They drank a lot and both of them got quite drunk. It helped ease the knowledge of their parting. It was only ten o'clock when they fell in the door of the Inn, giggling. They ran upstairs after getting their key.

The next morning they woke at dawn, sunlight shining directly through the now uncurtained window above their bed. And looking at the mess of the room they burst out laughing. Their clothes making a trail from the door. The curtain, off it's rail, crumpled on the bed. The duvet, on the ground. And the two of them, lying on top of it. They realised they had hangovers and got back into bed, leaving the mess for later.

That day, they found it almost impossible to get up, knowing it was their last one. They phoned the airlines to confirm their flights from the phone beside the bed and both shed a few tears.

During breakfast Helen wrote her parents a quick letter and gave it to Joanna.

"Will you give this to Mum and Dad and tell them I'll be home for longer at Christmas than I'd planned."

"What do you mean?"

"Well, I'd originally only planned for the few days

surrounding Christmas. But now," she put her hand on Joanna's, "I'm coming for as long as I can get off work."

They went back to their room to pack their bags. It took a long time. They wanted to say goodbye in private.

Checking out, Joanna used a credit card for the hundredth time that week. She held it up to Helen and laughed.

"Thank heavens for a lucrative career."

Joanna handed Helen the keys of the car. "Will you drive?"

Helen went off to get the car. Leaving the bags in the hallway, Joanna ran as fast as she could to the flower shop around the corner and bought a single red rose. As she walked back to wait for Helen she realised she would never forget this time - these precious days. She smiled up at the sun - there - yet again.

When they put their bags in the boot she handed Helen the rose. Helen accepted it silently. There was nothing for either of them to say.

They had a few hours left before their flights and Helen decided to drive across Golden Gate bridge to Marin County.

"You absolutely have to cross the bridge. I know it's a touristy thing to do but really it's worth it."

Joanna smiled at her. She didn't care what they did, but as they approached the bridge she realised Helen was right. The bridge was the most majestic thing she'd ever seen. Powerful and authoritative in a way she didn't know anything could be. More overwhelming and certainly more beautiful than the Eiffel Tower or the Empire State. With streams of glinting cars -

continuous - like blood running through a vein. And just like that the bridge would be dead without them.

As Joanna looked back at it she said "This is the only time in my life that I've felt the word 'awesome' should be used."

They got out of the car in a place they didn't know the name of. It was a fishing village. They walked down a pier full of fishermen wearing baseball caps and checked shirts. It was as quiet as a library. Every word spoken could be heard on the far end of the pier. Joanna and Helen didn't speak. They held hands and walked slowly. They both felt as if energy was leaving their bodies as the time to part loomed closer and closer. Helen made an effort to be bright, buying funny notelets for Joanna who laughed wearily. Neither of them ate their lunch. Neither of them wanted to drive when it was time to leave. But Helen did, seeing how down Joanna was. They didn't even laugh when two young men eyed them up as they got into their car.

Everything after that was robotic movement - only when necessary. Bringing back the car. Checking in. Joanna's flight was first. Helen's three hours later. They sat, very close, not speaking, waiting for the last call for the flight. When it came they went to the barrier and both fought against their tears - Helen winning her battle - Joanna losing.

Helen kissed Joanna's tears away.

"Soon Joanna - soon. Keep thinking of Christmas. We'll spend every moment together."

"I know, I just don't want to go."

"Nor do I, but we have to. It's all going to work out. It has to. It has to." Helen was saying it desparately, almost as if to convince herself.

They were completely unconscious of the many

curious eyes studying them as they said goodbye.

Joanna walked through the barrier, showing her ticket, down a long passageway. Just before the corner she turned and waved. Helen waved back, crying freely now.

* * *

A middle seat again.

"Fuck, why didn't I remember?" she said to herself as she sat down.

She stared ahead fighting the desire to get up and run off the plane. Her breath became shorter. Her chest felt tight. She pulled at the neck of her sweater wishing she'd worn something cotton. The man beside her had been eating garlic. She felt sick. Her head was pounding. She gripped the arms of her seat rigidly, holding herself down. Feeling if she let go that she would actually explode out of her seat. She tried to think of good things but couldn't. All she knew was that they were going to be thousands of miles apart again. And that Helen was going to be with Laurent. She couldn't even think his name without it stinging her brain, her heart, her entire being. She clamped her eyes shut and miraculously her brain closed down. When she became aware again they were in the air. She didn't know if she had been sleeping or if she had blacked out. It didn't matter, her breathing had evened out.

She slept a lot on the flight - didn't eat, didn't watch the movie and simply ignored the people on either side of her. The winds were against them which made them late. She only barely caught her connecting flight, not even having time to stop at the duty free shop. She was glad that she'd asked Conor to collect her. He hugged her and bustled her into yet another new car asking her how she'd got on and taking it at face value when she said "Fantastic, I'm just exhausted now."

After picking up her car she went straight to work. Derek greeted her with a hug.

"Who's the blonde?" she asked about the tanned young woman talking to Maire in the outer office.

"She's American, volunteering her services for free for a few weeks!"

Joanna raised her eyebrows. "Is she any good?"

"I hope so - Maire is leaving." He said.

"What? Why?"

"She got a job in RTE."

"You're kidding? Why on earth does she want to work in RTE? Did you offer her a raise?"

"No."

"Why not?" asked Joanna.

"Firstly because I think she gets paid well enough and secondly - I think you should sit down for this one," he said sitting down himself, "RPC have put out their stuff to tender for next year."

Joanna sat down staring at him. "You're kidding." she said again.

"I'm not."

"Jesus Derek, they're our biggest client. Why? They've always been so pleased with us. The last production I did for them was great."

"They didn't think so Joanna."

"What?" she almost screamed.

"They didn't like it. They thought it was over the top - too fast - didn't give the viewer time to absorb the information."

"That's bullshit Derek, and you know it. If that programme had been any longer, the topic was so boring that viewers would actually leave before the end of it."

"I know that, and you know that, but whether we like it or not they're paying for it and we have to give them what they want."

Joanna sighed, feeling defeated. "Oh God Derek I've made a mess haven't I? They said all that to me but I just said that they were wrong and went ahead regardless."

Derek leaned towards her. "Joanna, I'm behind you on this one. It is a great video and they are wrong. We just can't afford to take those sorts of risks for 'art's sake' you know?"

"I know it Derek, but I hate it," she said looking at her hands.

He got up and put a hand on her shoulder. "Don't worry Joanna - we may lose them this year, but we'll get them back next year. We'll just have to tighten our belts a bit and get some more work in."

"I'm sorry Derek - really I am."

"Come on Joanna, we've been through worse. Where's all that optimism gone?"

"I left my op-tim-ism, in San Francisco" she sang.

Derek laughed. "How did it go?"

"Fine."

He didn't ask again.

She went into the outer office to congratulate Maire on her new job and to introduce herself to the American. She smiled at herself for noticing that Amy had a firm handshake.

* * *

She thought about Helen and how close they were. All the things they did and finally she began to feel positive, almost high, about their relationship. Especially as Helen rang her often, extravagantly, saying how much she missed her, how difficult she was finding it to spend time with Laurent.

The 'high' lasted a week. One week. Then the feeling came back to her. Every morning. And her head began to thud again. Worse, she began having nightmares. Nightmares where she was outside a locked glass door and Helen was trapped inside. They pushed and hit but couldn't break the glass. Then, even worse nightmares, where Helen was in the locked room making love with Laurent and she and Helen could see each other and Helen was crying. On those nights she'd wake - sweating, get up and pace the house, put on music, write in her jotter.

*It's an absolutely impossible situation and you know it. OK, so maybe she's having trouble with her man. Maybe she misses you as much as you miss her. Maybe she wants to be with you more? That's a lot of maybes now, isn't it? The fact of the matter is that she isn't here and you're not there. And face it - she's even sounding down on the phone now. She's finding it hard to get up in the mornings too. She's sad. You are making her sad.*

Derek was desperately trying to pick up new business. Joanna tried, and failed to help. Derek stopped smiling. Joanna stopped sitting in her favourite chair and churned out barely adequate work that bored her. The creative element had disappeared for her. It had somehow become a job. A job she had difficulty getting up for in the mornings and hardly cared if she left or not in the evenings. She was barely keeping her head above water.

Helen could hear it in her voice on the phone and feel it in the many letters. Letters that were now showing despair.

Helen was counting the days to Christmas too. To when she could see her lover-friend, be with her. Reassure her of her love for her. Reassure her of ... what? Her own confusion was growing daily. After her two weeks with Joanna, she felt she couldn't live without her. But Laurent? What about him. They were so new really. She'd never felt like this about any other man. But it was Joanna she missed. Joanna she wanted to talk to. Joanna she wanted to be with. No. She didn't want to leave Laurent. Not now. Not yet. Joanna too had become like air to Helen. But Joanna didn't know. All she knew was that Helen was with someone else.

Joanna barely made it to Christmas. Each day she felt as if she had less air in her lungs. Every movement became an effort. But there was hope. There was still hope. Helen was coming home soon. And with that thought she'd perk up and get through the days and nights.

Helen came home - just in time. Her parents collected her from the airport. It was the day before Christmas eve. Joanna waited for her at 'their' house.

Helen knelt in front of her, sitting as always in front of the fire. She took Joanna's hands in hers. And all four hands were shaking. Their eyes simply reflected what each was feeling.

## Chapter Nine

Christmas? They spent it in their 'home homes' with their families. And enjoyed it well enough, with the knowledge that they'd be back in their secret world the next day. Too many parties in Dublin. Too cold in Donegal. They went to a friend's house in Wicklow. In Aughavana - a place neither of them knew. And they brought with them everything that was them, that had become them. Laughter, tears, understanding, gentleness, passion. Not forgetting good wine, good food and candlelight.

Their silences were longer than before. Silences where each knew instinctively what was in the other's mind but were too afraid to ask. Too afraid to hear the thought aloud. As if, once said, would then be. Helen read to her at night. In flickering candlelight. Before they made love. But now, accustomed to their physical love, they would make love indiscriminately - day or night - anywhere and everywhere. So much, in fact, it seemed they were unconciously making up for time they would spend apart.

One day they were walking through the forest toward the river. The river that somehow didn't look Irish. American, they decided. A river where big strong macho men would career down in kyaks, they joked. They were talking about foreign places they'd love to visit. Helen had been to many countries already, with her father's job and then as a student, but wanted to see 'absolutely everywhere'. Joanna, to a lesser extent. She adored Ireland - its freshness - its age - its beauty. Helen talked of its peoples' attitudes - narrowness, so often. Joanna contradicted her, almost for the sake of it. She hated Irish people who lived away and criticised the country endlessly. Helen wasn't one of these people she knew, but she contradicted her anyway. Helen hit back.

"Well, what do you think people would say if they knew about this?" She gestured at their interlocked hands.

Joanna shrugged. "Maybe they'd be like Kathy."

"Don't be such an innocent Joanna."

"I'm not being an innocent" she bristled "but I do think that people who know us, love us, would not, could not, think this disgusting. Could not think this anything but good and right."

"Don't kid yourself Joanna," Helen said. "This society - or any other - is not full of Kathys. It's full of bigots."

"Surely not *full* of bigots," Joanna persisted. "I believe that more people are prepared to live and let live than we give credit for. Anyway what business is it of anyone how people love each other? Or how they conduct their sex lives once it's not hurting anyone?"

"None, none at all. But unfortunately people make it their business to impose their beliefs on others."

"Is that why? Is that why you have a problem with this?"

"I *don't* have a problem with this. And you know it. You know what my problem is."

"Are you sure that Laurent is the only reason?"

"I'm positive."

They heard voices ahead, in the clearing beside the river. Joanna put her hands into her pockets.

"Why did you do that, are you annoyed with me?"

"No." Joanna nodded toward the young family coming into view. Mother, father, two little boys and a baby.

"Jesus Christ Joanna, and you're the one preaching faith in our society to live and let live - if you won't even hold hands with me in front of these strangers, you haven't a hope. I couldn't care less what they think."

She reached for Joanna's hand, who moved away and snapped:

"Well *I care*. I care Helen. I have to live here and I care if I get all the negatives that this sort of relationship creates, without getting the pleasure of the positives."

"What are you talking about?"

"I refuse to have a label printed on my forehead. I refuse to be called names. I refuse to create problems for myself if I'm not going to have the pleasure of what that lifestyle offers."

Helen said nothing.

"If I'm not actually going to live with you," she

finished quietly.

When eventually Helen spoke, she said "Who says you won't have that ... pleasure?"

"Well, will I?"

"I don't know. I just don't know anything anymore Joanna. Please bear with me on this Joanna. Please? I need more time. I know that's not reasonable but I do. I need more time."

Joanna thought for a moment. She had promised Helen time. She took Helen's hand and put it in her pocket along with her own. "Compromise," she said and smiled.

"You know something Joanna? You complicate my life too much."

Joanna laughed."I complicate your life?" mock disbelief. "You complicate my life so much that I think I'll call you 'the Complication'.

* * *

One night, while Helen was reading to her, she began to think about Helen going away again - and never coming back. Staying with Laurent forever. She stopped hearing Helen's voice and blackness began to cloud her vision.

It spread like a bloodstain on a white bandage. Unstoppable, sharp. It came from the back of her head and pressed against her eyes - wanting to escape. Inexplicable blackness that made her cry and cry, uncontrollably. She could see nothing, hear nothing. But she could feel. Feel the dull thudding becoming more severe. For moments she knew nothing but darkness and pain. And then things, objects, began to come into focus. She could hear - a voice. Feel - a body.

She was curled up in the corner of their bedroom, on the floor. The voice and body belonged to Helen. She was holding her, saying her name over and over - "Joanna, Joanna."

"Helen?"

"Yes love, it's me. It's me. Helen. I'm here."

Helen's eyes were studying her - searching for something? She began to kiss away Joanna's tears. "Come to bed, you're freezing." She led her to bed, helped her in and pulled the covers over her. Then sat on the edge, rubbing the frown from Joanna's forehead.

"Are you alright? Do you know where you are? It's OK, don't talk. You just didn't seem to know anything for a while."

Joanna didn't answer. Couldn't answer. She didn't know where she'd been either. And pain was still seering through her head.

"Do you want anything? Painkillers?"

She nodded. Helen ran out of the room and came back with two glasses in hand. One with disprin, the other with orange juice. She lifted her head and made her drink the disprin. She took a mouthful of the juice herself. Then took her friend's hand.

"Helen. I'm sorry. I don't know what happens me."

"Shhhh my love - don't think about it." She placed the glasses on their locker.

"Do you want to sleep?"

Joanna nodded. Helen didn't know if she wanted her there. She'd only ever seen her in this state once before.

Joanna managed to read her thoughts and patted the bed behind her. Helen blew out the candle and got into bed, assuming Joanna's usual sleeping position. She curled into her worn-out friend's back, put one arm under and around her neck, grasping her shoulder.

The other around her waist, resting on her stomach.

Helen woke often - gently pushed back Joanna's hair to see if she was frowning in her sleep. If she was, she gently stroked the frown until it disappeared. Never waking her.

But it was only a few hours - of one night - of many. The other days and nights they made the most of. They talked a lot about their sexuality. Never coming to any particular conclusion.

"But I still fancy men," Helen said as they were making a chicken and pepper stir fry. She was attacking the wok. Joanna was chopping the peppers. Each had a glass of wine nearby. "Well that's not quite true. I don't fancy men in general these days - not since this started." She smiled at Joanna.

"But did you fancy other men when you were with Laurent at first?"

"No," she replied quickly. "Well, actually yes. Sometimes, when he was away. I mean, I wouldn't actually do anything about it. I might flirt a bit, but that was it." She grinned at her friend. It was like the teenage conversations they used to have.

"Well why don't you fancy them now so?" Joanna persisted, trying to push the point home.

"God, I suppose my life is so complex now I just can't afford to. It just never occurs to me." She looked up to heaven.

The point remained homeless.

Joanna had brought her paints with her and stood at the window in the front of the cottage painting the forest and the river, unrecognisably. Using blacks, reds and purples. The river always looked like blood, Helen thought, slightly disturbed, thinking of the beautiful picture that Joanna had painted of her in the summer. These paintings were so ... hard and angular.

* * *

There were eight hours left of the old year when they went back to Dublin. They were having a party for neglected friends in their house, as they'd begun to call it.

"Helen, I'm so glad you're going to be with me to bring in the new year. You know how important dates are to me. Thanks."

"I don't want to be with anyone else for it," Helen smiled, pulling sixpacks off the fast emptying shelf. And realised that she meant it.

"Will vol-au-vents and sausage rolls be enough?" Joanna asked.

"Let's get smoked salmon and brown bread as well."

"Good idea."

Helen watched her go over to the bread counter and got that 'catchy' feeling in her throat again. The one she could never describe.

"I'm going to kiss you in front of all our friends tonight - when the clock strikes midnight," she said as Joanna took aim and threw loaves of bread into the trolley.

"You are, my arse."

"No Darling. Your lips."

"Don't even think about it." Joanna replied, searching for salmon now. She turned. Serious. "You can kiss me in front of the whole world tonight if it means you'll give this thing a try."

Helen walked away. "Christ Joanna." She said under her breath.

Twenty people. Good friends. Great punch. Enough food. Music. At eleven Helen whispered to Joanna. "I have to ring Laurent - it's midnight over there."

"Use the phone upstairs." Joanna didn't want to meet her eyes, so she didn't. She wanted to get drunk. Two people had already asked Helen, in front of her, how the 'man of her dreams' was? And she had to smile supportively as Helen floundered with the answer, trying to evade or move on. And Kathy didn't bother asking Helen. She took Joanna aside to ask how were things between Helen and Laurent 'really'?

But Helen was there. And everyone was having fun. And she discovered that her ability to 'switch off' was better than she'd realised.

"... 5, 4, 3, 2, 1, HAPPY NEW YEAR".

Everybody roared. The patio doors were open and fog horns and bells and car horns were all roaring too. Friends hugged friends, lovers hugged lovers. And the two who were both friends and lovers, hugged everyone else before each other. Then Helen held the back of Joanna's head with both hands and kissed her firmly on the mouth. And drew away. A kiss that good women friends could get away with - just about. A kiss that was as undecided as Helen's mind.

"What does that mean?" Joanna asked.

"Nothing. It means nothing. It means happy New Year Joanna. That's all." Joanna looked at her coldly. "Please Joanna, don't do this. Don't push me."

"Push you?" She flamed. "Push you - this has been

going on for six months and I can't take it anymore. My foundations are crumbling Helen. I just can't take it."

She felt more desperate than angry as she raced out of the room - almost unnoticed.

When Helen didn't follow, Kathy tried to. She, as usual had noticed. But Helen said "No Kathy, leave her. She wants to be alone."

Kathy looked at her unblinkingly. "That's exactly what she's afraid of Helen - and you know it." Her face was expressionless.

Helen took her restraining hand off Kathy's arm sharply.

They left Joanna alone. And in a short time she felt controlled enough to return to the party.

She wouldn't look either of her friends in the eye - nor would she talk to them. But no one else noticed. She could turn a cold look into a warm smile as easily as switching on a light. In a way that people who didn't know her intimately thought they must have imagined the coldness. Helen rarely saw her like this - she hated it. It frightened her. She felt like a child with a disaproving parent. And therefore tiptoed around her. Saying little - communicating little.

It was one of the few times they misunderstood each other. The longer Joanna was left alone, the colder she became. What she really wanted was for Helen to say something immediately. Hard or soft. It didn't matter. Anything to break the tension she felt inside. But Helen was cautious. Always. She rarely said anything without thinking it through first. And so, although for the first time she was really considering leaving Laurent, taking the chance, giving it a go, Joanna didn't know because Helen didn't say it.

Joanna got drunk. Blasted. Everything was a lively

haze. Helen hardly left her side. Saying nothing - just being there. Eventually she persuaded her to go to bed, after making her drink a pint of water, over which Joanna complained bitterly. Like a child being forced to take medicine. She wouldn't be undressed. "I hate people taking off my clothes" she said as she crawled into bed, leaving her shoes on. Helen didn't bother reminding her that it was OK. It was Helen. She knew Joanna was aware of it. She pulled off her shoes and covered her with the duvet. Then sat stroking her hair back from her face. Joanna rambled and rambled - talked nonsense. About locked doors and such like.

Helen looked around the bedroom. Their bedroom. Sweatshirts and jeans belonging to both of them, tossed on the wicker chair in the window. Light from the street illuminated the bookshelves - cluttered with a peculiar variety of books. Salinger, Binchy, Hemingway, Joyce, Archer. And candles - on every resting place possible.They were rarely in the room at night without the candles lighting. There were paintings on the wall - a recent addition. All with the startling colours she found so disturbing. And one photo of Joanna and herself, sitting side by side - talking. It was a photo that anyone who looked at it for some reason looked away from quickly, as if they were intruding. But then would always look back at it. They loved that photo. Helen had got blow-ups for both of them. Hers was on the mirror in her bedroom in Hong Kong. Laurent's silence about it was noticeable.

The music was blaring in the sittingroom and her name was being called. Joanna was whispering now.

"What love?"

"I love you Helen."

"I love you Joanna - more than anyone else in the

world." She shocked herself by saying it. She'd never said it before. But she knew it was true. Joanna was drifting off.

"I'll be back soon." She disengaged her hand, lit a candle and went down to disband the party.

When eventually she did go to bed, Joanna was asleep. But even in her sleep she was aware of Helen and she wrapped one arm around her shoulder and the other around her waist, nestling her face into the back of her neck.

Helen cried.

Joanna woke early. The inside of her mouth was dry. And her head hurt. She was too warm. It took her a moment to realise that she'd slept in her clothes. Helen had left a glass of water beside her bed. Thanks Helen! What was the smell? Booze - the party - Oh God, the mess, all came to her as she knee stepped over Helen. She went into the sittingroom. Clean, spotlessly clean. Kitchen, same thing. Glasses on the drainer - washed. Big black sacks of bottles in the corner. Oven trays on the cooker - clean.

Helen must have done it, but when? She hardly remembered anything. It was beginning to dawn on her how drunk she'd been. She put four disprin in a glass, watched them froth up and then dissolve. Drank them and opened the patio doors. Fresh air was badly needed. She moved quietly, not wanting to wake Helen. She sat on the carpet just inside the doors. She remembered midnight. But then what? Dancing with Dermot. Gillian and Tony arriving late. Kathy talking to her. And Helen - always there. Prince. She could remember dancing wildly to Prince for ages - in the garden. Where she'd put the speaker. "Oh God. The noise must have been deafening." She made a note to apologise to her neighbours, on both sides.

She felt a sharp pain in the pit of her stomach and winced. She knew it was the beginning of her long overdue period. Ten days late. It was supposed to have arrived the day before Helen! Instead it was arriving the day before she left. She wondered why. And thought of psychosomatic illness as she showered. Sometimes she reckoned that all ailments and physical problems could be controlled by the mind. Other times she thought it a ridiculous notion.

Helen was asleep when she went, wet, into their room to find some clothes. She was lying on her back, the covers had slipped off one shoulder leaving her breast bare.

Her arm was thrown across to where Joanna should have been. She had never seen Helen look vulnerable before. But lying there, asleep, unaware of her audience, Joanna thought her vulnerable.

She pulled the duvet up to cover her.

When Helen awoke, she found a very pale Joanna lying on the couch.

"Got a hangover?" she asked, kissing her on the forehead.

"A hangover and a period."

"God, how awful. Do you feel rotten?"

Joanna nodded. "Did you clean up?"

"Yes. Me and Kathy."

"You're an angel. I couldn't have faced it."

"I'm going to take a bath. Will you come in and talk to me?"

Helen got into her steaming bath and Joanna sat on the lid of the toilet seat. With a foot-shaped sponge she squeezed hot water over Helen's shoulders and down her back. Every time the hot water trickled down Helen's back she stretched like a cat. They talked about the party. And didn't talk about decisions or choices.

As Helen got out of the bath, Joanna wiped the condensation off the mirror. She looked at her reflection, drips passing through it, clear and then hazy - so fast.

"I can't do it anymore Helen. You have to choose," she said to her disappearing reflection which looked surprised.

Helen said nothing and put a towel around her.

"Christ Helen, Laurent doesn't even know. He knows nothing. This man you claim to love so much doesn't even know. How can that be?" Her voice was rising. She was still at the mirror.

Helen screamed. "Don't talk about him like that. Don't talk about him at all. What he and I do is none of your business. *None.*"

Joanna turned to face her. She was stunned. "None of my business? What do you mean? Of course it's my business. Of course it's my business. I hate that you're with him. Always going back to him - coming from him." She was getting angrier. "Do you know what I hate most of all Helen? Do you know?" She was screaming too. Moving closer to her. "I hate discovering," she pulled off Helen's towel agressively, "that I've just kissed one of his fucking lovebites."

Helen looked at the fading marks on her breast. She reached out to touch Joanna. But Joanna backed away and went into the garden where she knew she couldn't be followed immediately.

The garden didn't take much pacing.

She couldn't help but think that if Helen were a man, this would never happen. She would never stay with a man who was going back to another woman all the time, would she? No - no bloody way. So why was she doing it with Helen?

Helen came out. "I hate it too Joanna," she said softly. "I hate all the switching from one to the other. Tomorrow terrifies me Joanna. Leaving you, going back to him - having to switch - I hate it too. And I hate that he doesn't know. That he doesn't know why sometimes I can't make love with him. That he doesn't know why I'm crying sometimes. He thinks he knows, but he doesn't. And it's all so wrong."

"Then stop doing it."

"Joanna, you know it's not that simple. I love him too Joanna - don't you understand that I love him too."

"How can you love two people like this? It's not possible."

"Oh God - I don't know how. I just know that I do."

"You love him as much as you love me?"

"Oh Joanna, it's not a matter of *how much* I love him and *how much* I love you, it's ..."

"Yes it is Helen. It's exactly that."

"Oh Christ Joanna I'm so confused. It kills me that I'm hurting you so much. I don't want to hurt you."

"Then stop doing it."

Helen bent her head.

"I've decided to tell him."

"Tell him and then what?"

"Well, tell him. That's all."

"I want you to leave him."

"What?"

"I said that I want you to leave him."

"Leave him? Now? I can't," she replied as if it were an incredible request.

Joanna looked at her for the first time since she came into the garden. "OK, don't."

"What do you mean 'don't', what are you going to do?"

"Nothing at all. I won't be here for you though. You may as well throw it all out the window. The whole lot." Her voice was emotionless.

"Please Joanna. Don't do this. please?"

"Don't do what?" She said it like a parent speaking angrily to a small child. "I'm not forcing you to do anything. I'm simply telling you that I cannot do this anymore, and obviously I want you to choose me."

There was complete silence for a while. Well, silence that is, between the two women. The usual noises of cars and birds and general living were still going on. The rest of the world didn't give a damn about the dilemma the two women were faced with.

"I'm going to get the paper." Joanna left the garden and the house.

Her thoughts were going so fast she couldn't really grasp any of them. Did she mean it? Would she really leave Helen? But what would she do without her? What would she do? "I'm not going to neglect you anymore. No matter what happens," she told her house when she got back.

Helen was in the garden. Red-eyed and shaking. With the cold? Joanna began to feel sorry that she'd said anything. Sorry that she'd upset her friend. Her friend who was used to being happy. Should be happy. Her friend who didn't have blacknesses in her head. Yet.

She sat beside her, wrapped her in her arms and

began to rub her warm. "Let's go inside."

Helen didn't move. She whispered something Joanna didn't hear.

"What?"

"I'm leaving him." She started to cry.

She cried a lot that day. And that night. Joanna didn't know how to help her, but Helen asked her to stay and hold her, not to go out of her sight. And Joanna held her, while Helen grieved the death of one relationship and for some reason did not, could not, would not, celebrate the birth of another.

* * *

Helen was to return to Hong Kong and tell Laurent. Joanna promised to visit as soon as she could. And in the summer Helen's contract would be up, so she would come home and decide what to do, where to live. Everything.

That was the plan.

It didn't ring true. Not to Joanna. She wrote to Helen giving support and assuring her of how much she trusted her. Not the same words she wrote in her jotter.

*So there we go kiddo. Got your way.*

*Or did you? She didn't seem too happy - did she? Seemed pretty unhappy to me. Seem unhappy to you guys? You bet.*

*You don't really think she'll go through with it now do you? Oh God be sorry for you, you probably do, somewhere in the back of that innocent little brain of yours.*

*Think about it, just for a moment. What have you got to offer?*

*Love? Ha, love. They say (who 'they' are I don't know)*

*but anyway, they say that 'love conquers all'. Well in my view 'love conquers Fuck All'. But really, what are you offering her? A difficult life is what. A life living as ... come closer, I don't want to say this too loud ... lesbians.*
*Cop on!*
*She has this gorgeous guy in the palm of her hand. And they're still new. New and lovey dovey. They're nowhere near stale yet. It's a cushy setup.*
*Think on!*
*Sure she loves you. Sure she does. But what would she tell people? If anything. And when you think about it, you make her pretty damned unhappy don't you? Yes indeed. Pretty unhappy. He gives her love and affection, protection and support. I know you do too, don't jump down my throat. But you come along with doubts, fears, tears annnnnnnd a COMPLICATED LIFE!*
*Face it, why would she, or anyone else for that matter, give up something so lighthearted, for something so heavy-hearted?*
*Da naaaa. I rest my case.*

All she could do now was wait.
The call came the next day, near midnight.
Helen had told him. It had been awful. She was crying. He had said he wouldn't accept it unless she could say she didn't love him.
"I can't say I don't love him because I do." She cried.
Joanna tried to comfort her but she could see no light.
"I can't leave him like this. He's crying all the time."
It was then that she knew. She knew her friend would never leave Laurent to go to her. Never. It was then she knew that even if Helen and Laurent grew apart she would never make a life with Joanna. No

matter how much love there was. With fierce force she realised that for Helen, their relationship, including this new physicalness, could only be an experience *within* life - not something she could do *for* life.

And standing with the phone to her ear, saying soothing things to her lover-friend, she suddenly felt very foolish.

The realisation was there, but not the acceptance. Within a week of Helen 'leaving' Laurent, they were back together again - enhanced by their fragility and new-found transience. And Helen pleaded with Joanna not to leave her. She pleaded for more time.

Joanna broke her promise to her house. She felt no warmth, no welcoming when she came home in the dark evenings. They talked and wrote often - she and Helen. But it was all falling apart. They could only talk and argue about the unresolved situation. Helen was coming home for the summer. Definitely. Then she would decide. She promised.

They would meet alone first, for a holiday. As soon as term ended.

# Chapter Ten

"Wa da da di di bum bum beeeeep - it's eight o'clock and this is the news read to you by Michael O'Neill."

"Oh shut the fuck up Michael." She turned over onto her stomach, covered her head with the pillow and drifted back to sleep.

"Bleep bleep, bleep bleep, bleep bleep, bleep bleep, bleep bleep." She stretched out her arm, pulled the travel alarm off the bookshelf and switched it off. It read eight thirty am.

"Oh Christ, I'd better get up. Another bloody sunny day and I have to work." She walked naked to the mirror. "You are an ugly cow," she accused her pale reflection.

She pulled on her robe and went downstairs to face the day.

"Shit, too late to shower" she thought, looking at the kitchen clock. She ran into the bathroom - washed - brushed her teeth - tossed her hair with her hands - shook her head.

Into the kitchen - up with the ironing board - press dark jeans and navy polo - put them on - upstairs to find other leather boot - downstairs again.

Briefcase, keys - into car - start engine.

"Damn - forgot my bleep."

At last, she slammed the front door - hard.

Pulling out into the early morning traffic, cursing the jam which spread all the way down the road, wishing the clock back twenty minutes.

In the office she threw her keys on the tray.

"Hi there" Amy said, smiling at her. She'd got the job!

"Hi Amy, any messages?" she asked, picking up her pile of post, still walking.

"Just Gerry to check if you're still editing at nine thirty - I sent a message on your bleep," she shouted after her.

Joanna pulled the black miniature message machine out of her pocket to check for the flashing red light, dropping envelopes on the floor as she did.

"Fuck." There was no red light - she'd forgotten to switch it on. She had also forgotten the edit.

"Tell Gerry I'll be with him in a minute." She collected her tapes from the store room and dashed back past Amy.

"Joanna, Joanna come back - what about the costing for Monalex?"

She thought her head might explode as she dropped her tapes on Amy's desk momentarily. She sighed loudly. And thought fast.

"OK, we'll work through lunch and I'll leave him with stuff he can work on without me - I'll try to get to it at three thirty. We can courier it over by five thirty OK?"

Amy nodded.

"Will you set it up for me on the WP?"

"Sure" Amy smiled again. She was getting used to the routine.

"Are you sure that's right Joanna?"

"What?"

"Are you sure that part of the interview goes in there?"

She dragged her eyes back into focus and checked her script. Then started laughing.

"Christ Gerry, I'm glad someone's on the ball today." He swung around on the high-backed swivel chair, hands poised above the multitude of buttons and lights that glowed and flashed in the small dark room. His fair cheeks were spotted red from the heat produced by the humming machines.

He laughed too. "You'll turn me into a director yet."

The edit ran late along with her whole day. She barely got the costing out on time. She cleared her desk and decided to take her work home. She opened the back doors and started to clean the messy kitchen - getting dinner ready at the same time. She knew she must be hungry. She hadn't eaten all day. Fried fishfingers, an egg and bread. Then sat in front of the TV.

At nine she snapped awake to the sound of the telephone. Kathy. She was late for collecting her. She ran out of the house unshowered, work not done, unchanged and spent the night in the pub talking but not concentrating, listening but not hearing, and drinking a couple of drinks more than usual without even noticing. None of her friends could pinpoint what was wrong with her - just that she wasn't quite herself. But she was herself. She was exactly herself and it scared her. It scared her half to death. She was incapable of enjoying anything. And her eyes always felt so very heavy, as if they were only half open.

She left the pub early, her eyes stinging and her clothes smelling from the smoke-filled noisy room. She called in 'home home'. Her mum, Conor, Janine and Simba were all sitting around the fire having supper. She could see them through the front window and she stopped to watch them. They were eating cheese and crackers and pouring tea from the big brown teapot they'd had as long as she could remember. Her mother was holding court, her hands waving around almost wildly. Conor and Janine were laughing. She couldn't see her mother's face but she knew her eyes were crinkling and sparkling. Simba lifted himself up lazily - front legs first and moved away from the fire to settle on top of Janine's feet.

Slowly, she put her key back into her pocket and walked back up the drive.

For the first time in her life she felt out of place in her family home.

She drove back to her own house feeling lonely and empty. Thinking, thinking, thinking.

Recently she had noticed a coldness in Helen - one she'd never seen before. And when aimed at her, it chilled her. She heard it on the phone and saw it in her letters. Her voice became clipped and sharp.

"Look Joanna, we're just going around in circles. I've

told you I can't decide or choose. I've told you I don't know what I'm going to do. So if you can't handle it, that's your own problem."

Sometimes Joanna would respond with tears - sometimes anger - sometimes silence.

If it was tears Helen would immediately be sorry. "Oh God Joanna what am I doing to you? What am I doing? I'm destroying you. I'm so sorry. I just don't know what to do." And then she'd be crying. "Oh Joanna I love you so much. So much. I'm sorry."

And Joanna would try to comfort her. "Helen, *I'm sorry. I'm* sorry. I can't seem to help myself going on at you. I don't know what's wrong with me. Let's calm down and talk about something else."

And they'd hang up feeling drained but close.

If it was anger they'd shout at each other. Things they'd never say to anyone else.

"Christ Helen, you're so fucking selfish. You never think of anyone but yourself."

"And you're so bloody accusing. It's always my fault, isn't it Joanna? Never you. No, you couldn't be at fault for anything?"

"Well you're the one dangling two people at the end of a string - not me."

"*I am not* dangling two people at the end of a string. You have a mind of your bloody own - use it. I don't control either of you."

"I'm really beginning to wonder why I love you at all."

Then they'd slam down receivers feeling taut and strained and frustrated. Helen would put on her runners and go for a run. Joanna would slam her door, jump into the car, open all the windows, turn the music up full volume and drive - long and fast. Both returning within a couple of hours to write - apologies, explanations, whatever.

Silence was the worst. Because then they'd have nothing. But there were other calls.

"Joanna?"

"Helen, I'm so glad to hear you. How are you?"

"Missing you," she'd say softly. "Missing you a lot."

And they'd speak tenderly, so tenderly. And the vast distance would miraculously disintegrate for just a little while.

They'd go to bed on those days or nights feeling warm and both put pen to paper. Helen in Hong Kong. Joanna in Dublin. And they'd write. Beautiful letters. Letters for nobody's eyes but their own. Letters sometimes so similar they could have been written by the same person.

But it wasn't enough. Not nearly enough. Too much coldness was passing between them. They didn't know what to do with this huge love of theirs, never mind how to save it.

* * *

They never did go on that holiday - Helen and Joanna.

They went instead for a week in the west - in secret. Why? Firstly because Helen's flight was coming into Shannon. Secondly because Helen decided she couldn't bear all the misery anymore. Couldn't bear hearing Joanna so sad. Couldn't bear their arguments. Couldn't bear hurting Laurent so much.

On that day she told Joanna. Told her she wanted to stay with Laurent. He never pushed her. Never demanded anything of her. Never made her choose.

She didn't want to see Joanna.

Didn't want to touch her.

Didn't want to live with her.

She didn't love her.

And Joanna, slumped over the telephone, tears streaming down her face could only ask over and over "Why?"

Eventually she snapped and screamed, "You bitch, you don't even have the decency to say it to my face - you're a fucking coward. You're chicken shit scared to live with a woman. You and your fucking talk of liberalism and feminism. You fuck up my life and walk away." She was crying hysterically.

"Alright Joanna. I will come home. I'll come home and say it to your face."

* * *

Two weeks later Joanna sat in Shannon airport gazing at the green screen above her head. "EI 102 London 14.45 ARR" flashed off "Landed 14.51" flashed on. The clock read two fifty five.

Her eyes went back to the glass doors that were quietly sliding open as people came through laden with trolleys and duty free bags - eyes flicking to find their loved ones, waiting, mostly excitedly. She saw Helen first. Her eyes too flicking then landing. She dropped her bag and they hugged. Both of them were shaking - as usual - this time they didn't know why.

They drove without talking. They listened to music and Helen didn't put her hand under Joanna's thigh. Just once she reached out and touched Joanna's hair - pulling her hand away quickly, as if she'd done it by accident. Joanna acknowledged nothing. She was thinking about how she'd woken a few days before at dawn. Listening to the birds and watching the first light through her unlined curtains, acceptance finally came. Helen would leave her. Even if she stroked her hair and couldn't say 'I don't love you Joanna', even if they made love, even if they laughed and talked endlessly, she knew Helen had to leave. That was her choice.

Joanna didn't know why she had made that choice, but she had, and Joanna had to accept that she herself was not the one doing the choosing.

Maybe Helen couldn't live with another woman. Maybe she loved Laurent more. Maybe their love was too 'all consuming' for her to live with.

Maybe, maybe, maybe.

## Chapter Eleven

The sun *was* shining as she drove back to Dublin. No music. She felt astonishingly calm as she noticed a plane flying overhead - presuming it was Helen's plane.

"Joanna? It's Kathy."

"Oh hi Kathy, how are you?"

"Fine. How about you? Really Joanna, how are you? Please don't put up a front for me. Not at this stage, please."

"I'm not. I really am OK."

Kathy didn't believe her. "Would you like to go out for a while?"

"No thanks, I'm not in the humour."

"Well, will I come around then?"

"No - thanks but I just want to go to bed."

Kathy had never heard Joanna so ... bland. So dull-sounding.

"OK so, will you meet me for lunch tomorrow?"

"Sure Kathy, that's a good idea. I'll ring you from the office in the morning."

She lit candles all over the house and turned off the lights. She had a mild headache but didn't bother taking anything for it. And she sat listening to music. Their favourite music. She was thinking about nothing. But images kept flashing behind her eyes, like a silent movie. Sometimes in slow motion. Sometimes distorted. Images of Helen and herself together. Sunburnt and laughing. Driving and talking. Dancing. Shopping. Crying. Making love.

None of the images reached further than her head. One of the candles flickered out. It was pitch outside. She looked at the clock. Two am. She'd been sitting there for almost five hours. In her bedroom she pulled off her sneakers and jeans, leaving on her knickers, T-shirt and socks. and as she fell into an almost deathlike sleep it occurred to her that she'd forgotten to brush her teeth.

She woke late feeling stiff and hot with a terrible taste in her mouth. Her dull headache everpresent. She rolled over and fell to the ground on all fours, knowing it was the only way to get herself up. She was determined to get through this day.

Amy greeted her brightly in the office.

"Welcome back Joanna - have fun?" she drawled through fiery red lips.

Joanna laughed. "Oh yeh - I had great fun."

Amy never asked personal questions. She was

business-like, friendly and distant. Joanna was grateful for that.

"Derek's away today" Amy continued, ignoring Joanna's tired laugh, "He's given me loads of stuff for you."

"OK so, let's get to it."

Amy began her list.

Joanna drifted away.

She felt a hand on her arm. Amy's. "Joanna, we can do this later if you'd prefer."

Joanna looked at her sharply, wondering had Derek told her anything. But all she found was compassion, not knowledge, in Amy's eyes.

"No Amy. We must do it now. I must." She said it desperately.

And Amy went through everything clearly and slowly, checking that each item had sunk in before moving on to the next. Making suggestions when she saw Joanna having difficulty with decisions. When they had finished Joanna scribbled a number on a yellow notelet and handed it to Amy saying "Will you ring this number. It's my friend Kathy. Tell her I'm caught in a meeting and won't be able to meet her for lunch."

Amy took it, nodded and left the room.

She spent the next hour planning out her week. Every hour of every day. Every call she had to make. Every single thing. She wrote in thick red marker so that the writing stood out significantly in her diary. That day she tediously ticked off everything as she did it. Psyching herself up for each call before making it. And when Amy rang through with calls for her she'd tell her to take the number and she'd call them back. She did call them back. Each one. But only when she was ready. Helen never left her mind. But she was calm. She was calm.

It was seven o'clock when she finally cleared her desk. Amy was still there. She was on the telephone talking rapidly and obviously annoyed, pushing her hand along her newly spiked blonde hair.

"But yesterday you quoted me £339, I asked you to book them then. It has nothing to do with me that you didn't do it. You can pay the extra because believe me I have no intention of paying it, OK?"

Joanna sat on the edge of her desk. Amy looked at her and rolled her eyes. Within a moment she had slammed down the phone on the unfortunate travel agent on the other end.

"Sometimes you Irish really get to me." She had her head in her hands. She laughed then and looked up at Joanna.

"You look tired Amy. Go on home. Everywhere is closed now anyway."

"And that's another thing. Everywhere closes. You can get nothing done in the evenings."

Joanna said nothing. Amy looked at all the bits of paper on her desk despairingly. "Oh to hell with it."

Joanna dropped Amy to her bus stop. She noticed the two men waiting there gaping openly at Amy's long, well-tanned, well-shaped legs getting out of the car. Joanna laughed.

"What are you laughing at?" Amy asked, oblivious to the men. Or maybe just igoring them. Joanna didn't know which. In fact she didn't know Amy at all. Not the first thing about her.

She didn't tell Amy what she was laughing at, and

drove off forgetting her immediately, seeing a dark silky head in the car beside her. For a tiny moment she thought it was Helen.

It was something she was to get used to over the next few months.

Oh she knew Helen wouldn't be back. Yet couldn't help but look for Hong Kong post marks on the letters that fell on her floor every morning.

None ever came.

Sometimes the phone would ring late at night and go dead when she picked it up. She always wondered was it Helen, calculating quickly what time it would be in Hong Kong. And once she picked up the phone shakily and dialled Helen's number. She held the receiver tightly in both hands and shut her eyes when it was picked up after three rings. She didn't know what she would say as she waited to hear Helen's voice.

"Hello - Helen and I are not available right now. Please leave a message after the tone and we'll get back to you as soon as possible ...........beeeeeeeep."

She hung up and fell to the floor crying. She hadn't cried since Helen had left almost four months ago.

She cried herself to sleep on the floor of her sitting-room and woke a few hours later shivering with cold and exhaustion. She didn't make it into work that day.

Soon her phone stopped ringing at night and she never dialled the familiar 16/852 Hong Kong code again. And around that time Joanna packed away all Helen's letters, presents and photo's. She forced herself to read the letters first. One by one. From the beginning of the affair to the end. And even then she couldn't understand why it had all fallen apart. The progression was apparent in the letters but not the reasons why. Nothing made sense to her. How could there be so much love and then nothing? How? Nothing except all these memories and constant painful reminders of what she couldn't have. She cried exhaustedly as she zipped the full tube bag over their 'special' photo.

She gave the heavy bag to Kathy saying, "Put these somewhere safe Kathy please. Don't tell me where they are. And don't give them to me, even if I beg you. Not for at least a year." The bag also held the letters Joanna had been writing to Helen every day since she'd left. Her mourning period was over. She thought.

* * *

Slowly she began to socialise again. It was difficult, having to explain where she'd been for the last few months, using work as an excuse as usual. Even more difficult when friends asked "How's Helen? When's she coming home?"

Joanna would smile with broad lips and dull eyes and say "You know I never thought Helen and I would grow apart, but it's so difficult to keep up a friendship over such a distance!" Soon it was accepted and the questions stopped.

Helen's parents never called Joanna and she was grateful. Helen must have told them something. And one evening as she was walking with her mother on the strand - no Simba, Simba had died - she decided to tell her. And she sat on a bench crying in her mother's comforting arms, arms that hadn't held her since she was eight years old. Her mother asked her to come home to stay for a while, but Joanna said no. She needed to get through this thing alone. That evening going in her own front door she reminded herself to replace the bulb in the outside lamp. It had blown months before.

She also told Derek.

He had managed to rustle up enough work to keep them going and they were back on target again - no thanks to her.

"I wish you'd told me earlier Joanna. I really thought we were losing you and I couldn't understand why," he said.

"And do you now?" She asked "Do you understand now?"

"Yes" he said gently, tossing her hair.

She found it easier to work now that Derek knew. When he saw her under too much pressure he'd make her ease off and delegate her work for her. Taking on a lot of it himself.

"Derek, you're working too hard. Take a holiday," she said when she noticed him paler than usual, his laughter lines deeper now, even without a smile.

"Look who's talking," he replied.

"I don't need a holiday - I need a new life."

"You and me both."

"Seriously Derek, why don't you go while the new edit suite is being installed. We're going to have to semi-close anyway."

He said nothing.

"Where has Claire always wanted to go?" she asked.

"Scotland actually" he laughed. "For the first time in our lives we can afford to go almost anywhere and Claire wants to go to Scotland."

"OK, you're on your way. Two weeks in Scotland in September."

"Hang on a second Joanna, I can't leave you here

with the installation going on ..."

"You can and you will Derek. You've been carrying the can for me long enough now." She put her hand on his arm. "Please Derek - for me?"

Eventually he agreed.

She picked up the phone and asked Amy to organise a 'fabulous holiday' for Derek and Claire in Scotland.

September came and Derek went. English engineers buzzed around the office. Gerry was in his element - looking over the shoulder of each English accent. They were unofficially closed but Joanna and Amy were busy scriptwriting and handling an endless stream of phonecalls.

"Jane, come back - all is forgiven!" Amy laughed one afternoon as five telephone lines flashed in front of her.

At night Joanna treated all the hard workers to meals out - 'on the company'. It was expected occasionally but they were having such a good time showing the engineers Irish nightlife that they got caught in a social spin for two solid weeks.

"To the new edit suite, and to all of you for putting her into action." Joanna said as they raised their glasses of champagne the night before the English crew were due to leave.

Dave, who was senior in rank and age, raised his glass and said, looking at Joanna "To the best, most hospitable, best-looking clients we've ever had."

"Here, here" the other two chorused.

It was the first time Joanna had noticed how attractive Dave was.

None of them went to bed that night. They danced until the night club closed and then all six of them went to the airport. As they were saying goodbye, shaking hands and kissing cheeks, Dave kissed Joanna on the lips. She looked at him startled.

He grinned "I've wanted to do that since day one, but we're always told not to kiss our clients." He turned and walked through the barrier before she could say anything.

Amy and Gerry were laughing.

"I was wondering when he'd get around to it." Amy said.

Joanna looked at her amazed, "But I didn't even know he was interested."

"He thought you were playing hard to get!" Gerry said.

"What?" she said incredulously, turning sharply to try and see him before he disappeared. He'd gone.

That night Kathy called around while she was on the phone to Conor.

"Thanks Con," she said motioning to Kathy to make herself a cup of coffee. "I'll see the two of you on Saturday night so ... bye."

She followed Kathy into the kitchen.

"What's the tape Joanna?"

"It's a group called 'The Four of Us' - they're Irish," she said as the loud beaty music played in the sitting-room.

"It's a change from your usual mellow female vocalists." She raised her eyebrows at Joanna.

"Oh don't go reading anything into that. They're a good band." She poured herself a cup of coffee.

Joanna invited Kathy to Conor and Janine's anniversary party on Saturday night and told her about the three English guys - particularly about Dave.

"You don't know how good it is to hear you like this

again Joanna."

"Like what?" Joanna asked.

"In good form," Kathy replied simply.

* * *

But she still woke in the middle of the night with nightmares. All of them involving Laurent and Helen somehow. Helen appearing at a party, Laurent always looming up behind her.

Helen in bed with her - Laurent standing in the doorway. And as he appeared, Helen would leave.

Those nights she would wake, screaming, get up and write in her jotter until she fell asleep with her lamp still on.

*Get it together woman. This has to stop. It has to stop. She's not coming back. She didn't choose you. Live with it. Live with it. You had your chance. You gave it all. And she gave it back. It's not the end of the bloody world.*

But sometimes she thought it was, when she dragged herself out of bed in the mornings and only barely managed to go to work. She was up and down. And she wondered how long it could go on. This feeling of loneliness, of grief. She became angry at herself when every night she thought about Helen before she slept. Every night without fail. Remembering how they'd been. Imagining what Helen was doing now.

One night she tried to recall Helen's voice and found that she couldn't. She rubbed her face hard and went into the dark garden. The cold air didn't cool her down. She was burning. She pulled off her jumper and saw goosebumps on her arms, but she was still burning. She wanted to stop thinking. To stop her head spinning around. To stop the pain she felt inside every part of her. At every nerve ending. She sat on the wet grass and rocked herself.

"How long? How long? How long?" she kept asking aloud. "This is no life - no life. If this is all there is I don't want it."

She recognised the thought as real and she stopped rocking, ran into the house and rang Kathy. A sleepy voice answered.

"Kathy. It's Joanna. I need to talk."

Kathy was immediately awake.

"OK Joanna. Where are you?" She was matter-of-fact.

"At home."

"I'll be there in five minutes."

Joanna breathed out "Thank you Kathy."

"Joanna?"

"Yes."

"Don't do anything. Just wait for me."

"Don't worry, I'm not that stupid."

Kathy stayed with her that night and others. Calming her. Comforting her. Until eventually the days got easier for her. Very slowly, they did.

One morning at breakfast, Joanna beamed at Kathy.

"Do you know what I thought when I woke up this morning?"

"No - what?"

"Nothing. Nothing at all. My head was empty - blank."

She started to see her other friends. She started to spend time with her mum. But mostly she stayed in her house with her music, her thoughts and her loneliness.

Dave rang her from London.

"Hi, having any problems with the suite?"

She was glad to hear his voice.

"No - none at all. It's fantastic."

"Listen, I'm coming over next weekend for a couple of weeks - to work with one of your competitors."

"That's great."

"I was wondering could we get together?"

"Sure," she said. "Call in here any time."

There was silence for a moment.

"Dave?"

"Actually Joanna, I meant go out - you know - on a date."

"Oh" she said thinking quickly, "Sure to that too."

They met that Saturday night. Joanna didn't really feel like dressing up. She had to force herself to shower and change. Dave said she looked 'gorgeous' anyway. She was surprised at how easily they talked to one another.

They went out several of the fourteen nights he was there. He told her about his divorce and she didn't tell him about Helen. But she enjoyed him and all the attention he was giving her. As they were sitting down to dinner the night before he left, his hand brushed accidentally against hers and for a brief moment she felt that familiar, almost forgotten, physical shock one gets from the touch of someone special. She pulled her hand away sharply and sat far away from him that evening.

"I'd like to come back soon and see you," he said in Dublin airport the next day.

"I'd like that too" she said, not knowing if she meant

it.

He began ringing her often at work. She enjoyed their talks. But for some reason she was thinking more and more of Helen these days. And her dreams were getting worse. Now Dave and Laurent would be standing in the doorway together looking at Helen and Joanna together. She began to be afraid of going to sleep at night.

Dave came back two weeks later - just for the weekend - carrying a bunch of roses. She didn't like roses anymore. They reminded her of Helen and San Francisco. But she put them in water anyway. She had invited him to stay in her house. At the time it seemed to make sense, but the following morning when she woke she was sorry. It was only six o'clock. He was a silent sleeper. His long blond hair was splayed, partly on her pillow, now that it wasn't tied back in its usual pony tail. The bed was too warm. She wished for the coolness of her duvet on both sides but couldn't have it. Instead she got up.

With Helen everything had felt right. With Dave she didn't know. It didn't really feel like anything except 'pleasant'. She knew she shouldn't compare anything now to how it had been with Helen. Her logical brain told her that. But she couldn't help it. She put on Billie Holliday for the first time since she'd been in the West eight months ago and sighed.

She opened the back door and sat on the step. The breeze was cool but she liked it. She knew what she would say to Dave.

* * *

"Wa di, di, de, do, bum - beeeeeeep. It's seven o'clock and this is the news read to you by Michael O'Neill."

"Ha - I'm up before you today Michael," she said as she switched off the radio and ran downstairs already in her tracksuit.

"I'm going to paint you a different colour, Door," she said as she pushed her bike out in front of her. She had become used to counting the rotations of the peddals to keep her mind clear. Sometimes it worked. Sometimes it didn't.

There was a different gang of regulars on the early morning stint these days. But she greeted them all as she had the 'Conspiratorial Four'. These mornings she listened to the radio instead of cassettes. There were fewer reminders on radio. Not one day in the last two years had Joanna not thought about Helen. But it wasn't first thing in the morning or last thing at night anymore and somehow she felt that mattered. She had heard that Helen had married Laurent and they were still living in Hong Kong. The friend who unwittingly told her wondered was she unwell. She looked so pale. But that was almost a year ago.

She rang her mum before she went off to work to ask her to the theatre that night. She'd been given complimentary tickets to the Olympia.

"I'd love to Pet" her mother said. "Why don't you have dinner with me this evening before we head out?"

"OK Mum, I'd like that."

Derek was already in the office as usual.

"Hi Derek," she called. "Wanna cup of coffee?"

"Yes please."

They sat together drinking their coffee and discussing the week ahead.

"Oh yes Joanna - we're in with a good chance for the RCP account."

"Really?" Joanna was surprised.

"Yes. They called late on Friday to ask us in for a meeting. We're competing against two others," he said.

"I think maybe you should take Amy to that meeting." She laughed a little nervously.

"Don't be ridiculous Joanna." He smiled at her.

She had to go home before going to her Mum's that evening. She'd forgotten the tickets for the show.

It was a grey day. She sat in the traffic in silence and stared at the light specks of rain beginning to splatter on her windscreen, not turning on the wipers until the water began to stream. She smiled at herself suddenly, realising that she liked rain nowadays. It couldn't remind her of Helen - not after all their sunshiny days.

She still looked automatically for the Hong Kong postmarks on the hall floor every day when she opened her front door. Today was no exception. She looked. There was none. Suddenly the day she had bought the house flashed into her mind, so vividly she could almost touch Helen's hand as she recalled putting her spare front door key into it. And she wondered for the hundredth time if Helen had kept the key.

She picked up her jotter.

*What's a kiss? Easy.*
*A kiss is a physical exchange between two people.*
*What's the big deal about a kiss?*
*Well, it's a physical exchange between two people brought about by an emotional desire. Right?*
*What's so lovely about a kiss? That's another question.*
*Well, I suppose a kiss is an intimate, private, exclusive action shared between any two people who love each other.*
*Good grief Joanna, it took you long enough to find that out didn't it?*

THE END

A [illegible] el

# The Family Business 4:

## *A Family Business Novel*

*Carl Weber*

*with*

*La Jill Hunt*

***www.urbanbooks.net***

Urban Books, LLC
300 Farmingdale Road, NY-Route 109
Farmingdale, NY 11735

The Family Business 4: A Family Business Novel




ISBN 13: 978-1-60162-088-0
ISBN 10: 1-60162-088-8

Frist Trade Paperback Printing February 2019
First Hardcover Printing February 2018
Printed in the United States of America

10 9 8 7 6 5 4 3 2 1



Distributed by Kensington Publishing Corp.
Submit orders to:
Customer Service
400 Hahn Road
Westminster, MD 21157-4627
Phone: 1-800-733-3000
Fax: 1-800-659-2436

# Prologue

The glass doors of the quaint storefront situated in the Atlantic Terminal of the Long Island Rail Road read: NATE'S SHOE SHINE AND REPAIR. When the door opened, the brass bell clanged loudly and three men of different ages stepped inside. The older of the three, who was more salt than pepper, took a seat in the center of the three shoeshine chairs and made himself comfortable, while his two companions browsed around the store looking nervous.

"Can I help you?" a gentleman situated at the far end of the counter with his back turned to the men called out. He was working on a pair of cowboy boots that had to be worth a thousand dollars or more.

"Yeah, I'm looking for old man Nate?" the older of the three men asked. Unlike the younger men, he was wearing a suit. He had military dog tags hanging around his neck that looked like they'd been dipped in gold.

"You must not be from around here, 'cause my uncle Nate passed away almost ten years ago," the man replied, continuing to work without turning around.

"Sorry to hear that. Nate was a good brother," the man said sincerely. "So, what's your name?"

The man never looked up from his work. "My name's Joe, but folks around here call me Shoeshine. What can I do for you?"

"Get the fuck outta here! You're Shoeshine Joe. Man, you still the best shoeshine boy in town?" He laughed like they were old friends, lifting his shoe. "Man, how about a shine?"

"First of all, I ain't nobody's boy," Joe snapped angrily, still without moving his head. "Secondly, I'm the owner, so I don't shine nobody's shoes no more. We got a kid that comes in at four for the rush hour crowd that can help you with that." Joe stood up and finally turned around with a slight frown on his face.

Then he recognized the man sitting before him. He took a step back. "Shit, I thought you were dead."

"That's what I wanted people to think," the man in the chair answered, gesturing to his shoes. "Now, how about a shine for old time's sake?"

"Sure, sure, no problem." Joe hurried from around the counter and pulled out a shine box. The man eased back in his chair. "What's it been—five, ten years?"

The man ran his hand through his graying hair. "Closer to fifteen."

"Damn, has it been that long?" Joe shook his head. Observing the two younger men, he asked, "These your boys? They look just like you."

"Yes, sir, these two are the best parts of me, Ken and Curt." He pointed at his two sons. "Boys, Joe here is the best shoeshine man on the East Coast. Back in the day, every time I'd come to Brooklyn I had to bring three pairs of shoes just for him to shine. He's that damn good."

"Thanks, but that was a long time ago. It's been a while since I did this for anyone other than myself."

"Man, shining shoes is like riding a bicycle: you just got to get back on it," the man said, and Joe nodded his agreement as he began to apply polish.

"So, Joe, it looks like the neighborhood is changing a lot. How's business?"

"Changing is an understatement, but believe it or not, that's not such a bad thing, because business is good. These yuppies that are moving in don't wear two hundred–dollar sneakers like the old neighborhood folks. They wear expensive designer shoes and boots that need repair. Nobody wants to throw away a seven hundred–dollar pair of shoes, so for now business is better than ever."

The man glanced over at the two younger versions of himself, who were now posted at either side of the door; then he looked down at Joe.

"That's great. I'm happy for you," he said sarcastically. "But I wasn't talking about the shoe business. I was talking about the information business."

Joe froze, peering over his glasses. It had been years since anyone had even mentioned the figure he was now kneeling before. The man was a killer, no if, ands, or buts about it. Word on the street was that he'd been locked up and died in his jail cell, but that couldn't have been true, because he was sitting right there in the flesh, asking for information. Joe just hoped the information he wanted wasn't the kind that might get him killed.

"I don't really know much about nothing other than shoes." Joe shrugged as he tentatively continued to shine the man's shoes. "My uncle Nate was the one who knew everything about everyone. Not me."

"Is that so?" It was obvious from the look he gave his sons that the man thought Joe was lying through his teeth; however, he remained calm. He nodded to Curt, the older of his sons. Reaching into his pocket, Curt pulled out a stack of cash and placed it next to Joe's shoeshine box. It was more money than Joe had seen in a while.

"I'm sure you can be just as helpful as your uncle, don't you think?" Curt spoke for the first time.

Joe stared at the money, thinking of the pile of bills stacked on his kitchen table at home, along with the constant calls from the finance company about the past due note on his wife's car. It was tempting, but still, he didn't move.

"I'm sorry. I'm not big on information." He went back to shining the man's shoes.

"Okay, maybe *information* is the wrong word. The truth is, I'm looking to buy something. Maybe you can help me with that." The man reached into his pocket and pulled out another stack of cash, placing it alongside the money Curt had put down.

"Wha–what you trying to buy?" Joe asked nervously. He swallowed hard as he gathered up the bills and placed the money in his apron pockets. Glancing up at the two other men, he saw that they were amused by his sudden change of heart. Not that it mattered to him. He knew there had to be at least twenty or thirty thousand dollars in front of him, and it was a sum he just couldn't pass up.

"If I wanted to purchase a large amount of dope, where would I go to find it?"

"You're joking, right?" It was Joe's turn to be amused. "If anybody knows where to find dope, it would be you, wouldn't it? You know the key player better than all of u—" He stopped abruptly when the man bopped him on the head just hard enough to get his full attention.

"Motherfucker, don't worry about what I know. Does Verizon go to Sprint when they need new towers? Does Ford go to GM to help them build cars? Of course not! So why the fuck would I go to LC and ask for help? I'm trying to put his ass outta business."

Joe raised his hands defensively, hoping to give himself a moment to collect his faculties. That was not the response he'd been expecting. He thought for a second and said, "Well, you can't go to the Mexicans or the Colombians now that Alejandro's dead."

"Why not?" Curtis asked.

"Rumor has is it LC's son Vegas is fucking—or used to fuck—Alejandro's widow, and she's supplying them with everything they need. But there is always Lee and his people. He's been hurting ever since him and LC fell out over that Sal Dash fiasco."

"I never liked that Asian bastard, but it's worth a try. The enemy of my enemy is supposed to be my friend, at least until you kill the bastard." The man laughed. "All right, so who else you got?"

"Well, there is a guy who's been looking to move some product. He usually moves marijuana, but he's sitting on a shit load of dope, and I heard he wants to unload it cheap." Joe finished one shoe and moved on to the other.

"Why is he sitting on it?"

"Nobody will buy it from him. Guy's got a price on his head, and everyone is afraid of pissing off the Duncans. He's got a lot of dope, but his supply isn't infinite. Where do you go once he dries up? Not to the Duncans, that's for sure."

The older man sat back. He looked intrigued. "Sounds like me and him need to have a talk. What's his name?"

"Vinnie. Vinnie Dash."

He lifted his head. "This Vinnie any relation to Sal?"

"Yeah, he's Sal's son. He's the only Dash left after the war a few years ago. Which LC won, I might add."

"Is that right? So, where do I find this Vinnie Dash?" the man asked.

"You don't. Dude's running his business out of Jamaica. You gotta get in touch with his man Jamaica John in Co-op City if you want him. He runs a vape shop," Joe said matter-of-factly, getting over his initial discomfort now that the information was flowing.

"Okay. Thanks, Joe. For someone who doesn't know much information, you've been extremely helpful. Hasn't he, boys?"

The two younger men smiled and nodded.

"Glad I could be of service. Good doin' business with you."

"Pleasure was ours," the man replied as Joe finished off his shine. "I'm sorry we won't be able to do business in the future."

"Huh?" Joe was confused until he looked up and saw the gun pointed right at his head. Before be could react, a silenced shot entered his forehead and he fell to the floor.

"Damn, why'd you shoot him?" the younger of his two sons shouted. The older son didn't look happy, but he kept quiet as he picked up the money that had spilled out of Joe's apron.

"I wasn't taking a chance of someone paying his ass double what we gave him to tell them what we wanted. Now, help your brother pick up the money and let's go. We got business to handle."

# LC

## 1

*Grateful.* That was the only word that came to mind as I looked over the balcony of my bedroom into the sprawling backyard of our family compound. The sun was bright in the sky, but a slight breeze dissipated most of the morning heat. It was going to be a scorcher, that was for sure—not that the heat bothered me. I was just glad to be alive. It was a little less than six months since I'd been shot and left for dead, so no one appreciated a beautiful day and a little excess heat more than I did.

For a few minutes, I watched my grandson Nevada practicing his martial arts stances with his instructor, Minister Farah. At one point, he stumbled just a bit, but to his credit, he never lost his composure. I could see he was serious about perfecting the art. He would not quit until he got it right, like a true Duncan.

"Breakfast is ready."

I turned to see my wife Chippy easing up beside me. She was wearing a multicolored caftan and a pair of simple gold sandals. I had been so caught up in watching Nevada that I hadn't even heard her sneak up behind me.

"What's got you out here grinning like that?" She slipped her arm around my waist.

"Thinking about you." I reached over, pulled her close, and kissed her softly.

"Liar." She laughed and shook her head.

"And Nevada," I added, sliding my hands down to caress her butt.

"Mm-hmmm." She flirted, squeezing me back. "What were you thinking pertaining to me?"

I gave her a seductive look and said, "About last night."

"Yeah." She grinned. "Last night was pretty darn amazing and definitely worth smiling about."